kiss
IN THE DARK

ALSO BY LAUREN HENDERSON

Kiss Me Kill Me
Kisses and Lies

Coming in Summer 2011
Kiss Me Goodbye

Adult Fiction
Tart Noir (anthology, edited with Stella Duffy)
Exes Anonymous
My Lurid Past
Don't Even Think About It
Pretty Boy
Chained
The Strawberry Tattoo
Freeze My Margarita
Black Rubber Dress
Too Many Blondes
Dead White Female

Adult Nonfiction
Jane Austen's Guide to Dating

kiss
IN THE DARK

LAUREN HENDERSON

DELACORTE PRESS

Copyright © 2010 by Lauren Henderson
Cover photograph copyright © Jean-Bernard Adoue/Corbis

All rights reserved. Published in the United States by Delacorte Press,
an imprint of Random House Children's Books, a division of Random House,
Inc., New York. Originally published in hardcover in the
United States by Delacorte Press in 2010.

Delacorte Press is a registered trademark and the colophon is a
trademark of Random House, Inc.

Visit us on the Web www.randomhouse.com/teens

Educators and librarians, for a variety of teaching tools,
visit us at www.randomhouse.com/teachers

Library of Congress Cataloging-in-Publication Data is available upon request.
ISBN 978-0-385-73777-7 (hc)—ISBN 978-0-385-90690-6 (lib. bdg.)
ISBN 978-0-375-89588-3 (ebook)

ISBN 978-0-385-73778-4 (tr. pbk.)

Printed in the United States of America
10 9 8 7 6 5 4 3 2 1

First Trade Paperback Edition

TO RANDON BURNS, WHO'S SEEN ME FALL ON MY
BOTTOM ON A GYMNASTICS MAT SO MANY TIMES IT'S
PROBABLY SCARRED HIM FOR LIFE. AND TO RANDY,
DONNA, XAVIER, JEN, NOI, AND EVERYONE
AT ELITE GYMNASTICS: YOU WERE SO POLITE
ABOUT ME FALLING ON MY BOTTOM FOR YEARS.
I DO APPRECIATE IT.

Acknowledgments

To everyone at Delacorte Press, past and present, who has worked so hard to make the Scarlett Wakefield series a success, from the great editing to the lovely covers to the excellent publicity and promotion. I'm hugely grateful.

And to my agent, Deborah Schneider, and to Cathy Gleason, who works with her. They truly are always there for me, and I cannot thank them enough.

one

ME AND JASE AGAINST THE WORLD

We're running as fast as we can in the dark. Holding hands, our breath coming in quick spurts. Down a gravel path, the heels of our trainers crushing the stones against each other, sharp grinding noises each time we land and push off again. Onto tarmac, for a few short steps. Behind us a man is bellowing like an angry bull, and we know he must be chasing us, though we can't see him. Our ears are full of the yelling and the sounds of our own feet, our own breath, as we race away through the night.

And then, finally, grass beneath our feet. Open land. We're running even faster, in great lopes; if we were horses we'd be galloping. Cold night air on our faces, soft yielding soil below, on which we land almost silently. I think of werewolves in books, how they can race through forests so fast it's almost like flying, their paws barely touching the ground. That's how I feel as I run and run, my hand in Jase's, our strides matching each other perfectly even though he's much taller than me.

It's like when I'm running in my dreams, sprinting so fast

I feel I'm almost about to take off. Someone's chasing me, but they'll never catch me, because my feet are winged.

But even in my dreams, I've never run like this with Jase.

His father's yells are receding now, bare wisps of them carried on the air, reaching us across the stretch of untended grass that runs along the side of the barns. He tried to run after us, but we left him far behind. I picture him bending over, hands on his thighs, wheezing for breath, his face an apoplectic red.

Jase wheels and turns and I follow him effortlessly as he swings to the side of the last barn, ducks, dropping my hand, and pries away a loose board from the wall of the barn.

At first we were running blind. When Jase's father sneaked up on Jase and me kissing goodnight, shone a torch on us, and yelled all kinds of things that I never want to hear myself or Jase called again, we took off like startled rabbits, straight into the dark, only our knowledge of the school grounds saving us from running straight into a wall.

But by now, my eyes have recovered from the torch beam and grown accustomed to the dark. There's a waxing moon, a fat unfinished white crescent low in the black velvet sky, and thousands of tiny white pinprick stars; luckily for us, it's a clear night.

So I can see what Jase is doing as he lifts a second board away and props it against the side of the barn, making a gap wide enough for even him, with his broad shoulders, to clamber through. And I can also tell that out here it's as light as day compared to the pitch-black interior of the barn.

Jase is already halfway through, entering sideways, careful not to catch himself on a snag on the boards. He turns his head to me, his golden eyes bright even in the darkness, and holds out a hand.

"Scarlett?" he whispers.

But it isn't really a question. He knows I trust him. He knows I'll take his hand and follow him into the barn, even if the opening is as dark as the hellmouth and I have no idea what's waiting for me inside.

Right now, I think I would follow Jase anywhere he asked me to.

Because right now, it feels like me and Jase against the whole world.

I wriggle through the gap without any difficulty. Jase's hand is warm in mine, guiding me as I step cautiously over a board and onto the packed-earth barn floor. He snaps open his Zippo lighter, and a small circle of light around us shows me the looming yellow side of a tractor to our left. Beyond that is what looks like the big ride-on lawn mower that Jase and his dad use for the endless maintenance of the Great Lawn, tracing perfect green stripes up and down its length.

"This way," Jase hisses. He wraps his arm around me and guides me over to the back of the barn, where a wooden ladder is propped, leading up to sheer blackness.

I don't hesitate for a moment. I'm shinnying up the ladder before he can even tell me that's where we're going.

It's a hayloft. I crawl out onto the wooden platform and get a mouthful of the nasty scratchy stuff immediately; I'm coughing it out as Jase hauls himself up behind me.

"God, you climb like a monkey," he says admiringly. "One minute you were there, next you were gone."

"It's my special skill," I say, grinning, but he can't see me

3

smile. He couldn't climb the ladder with the Zippo on, and up here it's so dark I can barely spot my hand in front of my face.

I turn over to sit on my bum and wriggle back to make room for Jase, hearing him land on the floor of the loft. I don't manage it fast enough, though, and a second later he's almost on top of me; he must be on all fours. I hear his hands, his knees, padding on the wood, like he's a big animal coming toward me. I shiver from head to toe in excitement, tinged with more than a trace of fear.

Not fear of Jase. I could never be scared of him. But I'm a little bit scared of my own feelings. Of how excited he makes me. It's so powerful it's almost like something rising in my throat, almost like I'm going to be sick with the strength of my own emotions.

And no, that's not pretty. It's really raw. This is something that being with Jase is teaching me. Caring for someone as much as I care about Jase, wanting to be with him as much as I do, isn't like I thought it would be when I had huge crushes on pop singers and actors who played sexy vampires. Just last year, when I was still at my old school, St. Tabby's, my friends Luce and Alison and I were still obsessively collecting magazines with our crushes on the cover, Googling their names, sighing over pictures of them out running or on the beach.

And now there's a real live boy right in front of me on his hands and knees, his warm breath on my face, making my head spin with his nearness, and I'm feeling things I never, ever thought I could feel when I was giggling over magazines.

"Scarlett," he says softly. "You're right there, aren't you?"

Jase shuffles forward one more pace, trying to find me in the dark, so close that I don't even need to reach out to touch him. All I have to do is tilt my head ever so slightly forward, upward, following his breath like a vapor trail until my lips find his.

It's a light touch for a moment or two. Like it was when we were kissing goodnight in the courtyard just now, not wanting to get too carried away, a gentle farewell before I went off to finish my English homework for an hour or two before bed. And then all our pent-up frustrations explode, our anger at having to sneak around in the dark when we're not doing anything wrong, our humiliation at being caught like that by Jase's dad and the words he called both of us. Two seconds later Jase has grabbed hold of me and pulled me up so I'm on my knees facing him, and we're kissing as if we're drowning and going down for the last time.

He's squeezing me so tight it hurts, and I'm pressing myself into him till I can feel every inch of him, the zip teeth on his leather jacket, his belt buckle cutting into my stomach, his strong biceps wrapped around my chest. My hands slide down the back of his T-shirt, trying to feel as much of his smooth skin as I can.

I've never kissed Jase this passionately. I've only kissed two other boys in my life: once was incredibly romantic— before it went badly, horribly wrong—and once was what Miss Fisher, my terrifying Latin teacher, would call valedictory. A farewell kiss, saying goodbye to something that was over before it ever really began. Something that, for all sorts of reasons, could never, ever have blossomed into anything more.

So this kiss virtually shatters my world. I didn't know it

5

was possible to feel broken into pieces but so alive that every nerve ending in my entire body is sparking with fire. Jase throws his head back, groaning, and I twine myself even tighter around him, kissing his neck, his unbelievably smooth, musky skin. I'm thrilled beyond belief that it's me, Scarlett Wakefield, not seventeen yet and not exactly experienced, having this effect on him. Making him so crazy that he can't get a word out, just moans and gasps.

And then Jase grabs my face, his fingers twisting in my hair, pulling out my ponytail elastic, cupping the back of my head, his mouth coming down hard on mine. The sensation is so strong that I'm amazed I don't burst into flames.

Jase's tongue is warm and wet in my mouth as he insistently kisses me, and my tongue is twining around his just like our bodies are. This is faster, harder than anything we've ever done before, so intimate, so open that when Jase starts pulling up my sweater, tugging it out from between our bodies, I arch my back to let him have as much access as he wants, and I unzip his jacket and tug up his heavy T-shirt and when we press our almost bare chests against each other, more skin on skin than ever before, it's so exquisite that my breath catches in my throat and if I could see anything in the darkness, anything at all, it would be stars.

"There's a couple of blankets in the corner," Jase mumbles against my mouth. "I kip down here sometimes when Dad's cutting up so much I don't want to go home. We could lie down, get a bit comfier. I won't do anything you don't want me to do."

I totally believe him. But that's the trouble: right now, I

want him to do everything. Anything and everything. I can't ask Jase to be stronger than me; that would be completely unfair. It's myself I don't trust to keep me safe, because I want Jase so badly I'm scared I'll just keep kissing and kissing him till both of us are in way, way over our heads.

I want to lie down on some blankets in the hayloft with Jase more than I've wanted anything in my life before. More than I wanted to find out who killed Dan, the first boy I ever kissed.

And I wanted that very badly indeed.

I'm fizzing. I really am on fire.

"Whoa!" Jase jumps away from me slightly, though it's actually more of an awkward shuffle because we're on our knees. "You just buzzed me."

I look down at my sweater, pulled up to just below my bra. Zipped into its side pocket is my mobile phone, which I set to silent. It's vibrating madly to let me know that someone's ringing me.

Here's the very sad thing about my life: I don't have many friends. In fact, I only really have one. I lost Luce and Alison when I chose to hang out with the popular girls instead of staying loyal to them; I crossed a street and changed my entire life, and I don't blame them for not forgiving me for my betrayal.

And now that I've been buried alive at Wakefield Hall Advanced Security Collegiate Prison for Young Ladies, the school in the countryside that my grandmother runs with an iron fist in an antique-lace glove, I haven't made many new friends. It isn't easy, when your grandmother's the headmistress. Or when you can't confide in anyone about the truth of the circumstances behind your having to leave your old school and come here, because you were involved in the death of a boy you were kissing who dropped dead at your feet, and you've been utterly and totally forbidden to talk about it.

My only friend is called Taylor McGovern. She's American, tough as nails, and like me, she doesn't quite fit in to Wakefield Hall's highly refined, madly academic atmosphere. She knows all my deepest darkest secrets. Apart from Jase, she's the only person who might conceivably be ringing me at this time of night.

And since Taylor knows I'm out with Jase, she wouldn't ring me unless it was incredibly, mind-bogglingly urgent.

Which means I have to answer the phone.

"Sorry," I say to Jase, dragging the phone out of my pocket and hitting the Answer key.

"Scarlett!" Taylor says in a rush. "Look, I'm really sorry to be calling when you're on a date, but it's about Plum."

My heart sinks to the barn floor, a good thirty feet below me.

Plum Saybourne. My nemesis. Five foot nine inches of chestnut-haired, green-eyed, designer-clad evil incarnate.

This is going to be bad.

"She's got hold of this book she found in the school library," Taylor says. "Some kind of etiquette guide. There's pictures of you in it and she's showing them to everyone."

No no no no. This can't be happening. How could I have forgotten about that bloody etiquette guide?

"I'm coming straight back," I say grimly. "Where are you?"

"Pankhurst dorms," Taylor says succinctly. "Meet you at the front door."

I click the phone off. In its light, for a moment, I see Jase, his handsome face frowning in disappointment.

"I'm really sorry," I say sadly. "It's an emergency."

"Your aunt?" he asks.

"No. A girl called Plum. She's pretty much my sworn enemy."

"That posh girl with the furs and the Merc?" Jase pulls a face. "Snobby cow."

"Jase! *I'm* posh!" I protest nervously.

Jase Barnes's family has been the Wakefield Hall gardeners for generations, living in a tied cottage on the estate. While I'm Scarlett Wakefield, the heir to the hall, daughter of Sir Richard Wakefield. Jase and I haven't ever talked about it, but I think we both assume that the reason his dad is so against our being together is the huge class difference between our families.

"You're posh, but you don't look down on working people." Jase takes my hands. "That's the difference. You don't have a snobbish bone in your body. I've seen that Plum around a couple of times when I've been working in the grounds. She'll flirt with me, all right, but if someone like me actually took her at her word and asked her out, she'd sneer at him like he was dirt on her shoes."

Glad as I am to hear that Jase doesn't think I'm a snob, I can't help homing in on another part of this.

"She's flirty with you?" I say, my voice rising dangerously.

"Told me I had nice wide shoulders," he says, and though the phone light's gone out now, I don't need to see his face to hear the smile in his voice. "What, you jealous now?"

I am. Madly.

"You *do* have nice wide shoulders," I say, trying to sound airy and unconcerned.

"You don't need to be jealous, Scarlett." He wraps his arms around me. "You know that, right?"

This time our kiss is tender, reassuring. It would be lingering, but I break away because of the alarm bell ringing in my head.

"I've got to get back," I say regretfully.

"Okay." Jase lets out a long slow breath in a sigh of regret. "I'll stay here for a couple of hours, till Dad's had enough time to calm down and knock himself out with some more cheap whisky."

"Oh, *Jase*." I squeeze his hand. I'm an orphan, which isn't exactly a ton of fun, but whenever I think of Mr. Barnes it makes me realize that there might be worse fates in life. "Do you sleep out here a lot?"

"When he's on the warpath," Jase says. "He's always passed out by midnight, though. Then I can go back." He hugs me. "I'd walk you back to school, but if Dad's still out and about and catches us together . . ."

"No, better not," I say quickly. One encounter per evening with Mr. Barnes is pretty much my limit. "He won't bother me if I'm on my own. It's just seeing us together that gets him going."

Jase lights his Zippo to show me the way down the ladder,

holding it high, away from the straw. We've got more than enough drama in our lives already without setting a barn alight.

I hate to leave him. And I hate just whispering "Bye" as I make my way out through the gap in the boards.

Because what I really want to say is "I love you." The words are trembling on my tongue. I want to say "I love you" and then run away, really fast.

Just in case he doesn't say them back.

Two

AN ARMY OF PLUM-BOTS

I can't believe I forgot about the "Wakefield Hall Etiquette Guide for Students"! I'm thinking, furious with myself as I sprint across the field, vault over the stone wall, and land on the grassy verge of Lime Walk, back on officially sanctioned school grounds again. *Why, why, why didn't I get rid of it as soon as I realized I was coming here as a pupil?*

Because I was in such a state of misery that when I crawled back here, after I kissed Dan McAndrew and he promptly choked to death because of an allergic reaction, I was barely able to remember my own name.

And probably also because the entire etiquette guide episode was so horrific I just tried to purge it out of my brain as soon as I could.

A couple of years ago, my grandmother decided that the young ladies who comprised the current set of pupils at Wakefield Hall Collegiate were falling way below her extremely strict set of standards of conduct and deportment, despite having the aforementioned standards drilled into them every waking minute of their days. She attributed the problem to their home environments. Apparently, parents nowadays simply didn't know how to teach their children how to behave.

Her solution was simple and elegant. Who better than Honoria, Lady Wakefield, to put together a Wakefield Hall etiquette guide?

And who better, in her opinion, than her granddaughter, Scarlett, to pose for the photographs in the guide, demonstrating how to sit on a sofa, skirt demurely arranged over her knees; how to get out of a car, legs pressed together politely; and how to hold her cutlery correctly, fingertips never touching the tines of her fork or the blade of her knife?

Looking, in other words, like a complete and utter idiot.

Originally, my grandmother's idea was to send out a copy of the guide to the parents of every girl at Wakefield Hall when she started her first term. Miraculously for me, however, the move turned out to be one of her rare misjudgments. Her faithful secretary, Penny, told me in confidence that a large number of parents complained when the first batch of guides went out. Although some were apparently grateful for it, the vast majority was insulted by the presumption that they didn't know how to teach their daughters the proper way to hold a fruit knife while paring an apple.

Since it wasn't possible for the school to send out guides to some parents but not others, the "Wakefield Hall Etiquette Guide for Students" was retired from circulation after just one year. One year too many for me, but a whole lot better than having the wretched thing go out to every new girl at the start of the autumn term for the rest of eternity.

Nowhere in the guide does it say I posed for the photos.

And since I wasn't a pupil at Wakefield Hall then—it was assumed I'd stay at St. Tabby's until I was eighteen and went off to university—my grandmother firmly overrode my objections by saying that nobody at the school would ever identify me.

And they probably wouldn't have. After all, at fourteen I was still a skinny girl with her hair in plaits. A big difference between me then and me now, nearly seventeen, with boobs and hips and a bum (all a bit more sticky-out than I'd like, but I'm learning to live with them).

If someone as twisted and sneaky as Plum hadn't got her sticky fingers on it, my secret would almost certainly have been preserved.

"Knees *together* when you slide out of a car, ladies! That way no one can tell if you're wearing a thong or nothing at all!" comes Plum's high-pitched drawl, easily audible though I'm on the other side of the common-room door. "Personally, I think she's wearing granny pants, don't you? Or gym knickers. Big brown gym knickers to preserve her maidenly modesty! Because she's *definitely* a maiden, don't you think?"

A round of tittering laughter greeted this salvo of comic brilliance. Bracing myself—Taylor behind me, both of us having just sprinted up the main stairs of Pankhurst dormitory—I push the door open and step inside.

Jase thinks you're gorgeous, I tell myself for courage. *The handsomest boy you've ever seen thinks you're gorgeous and wants to kiss your face off. Be strong.*

But the scene inside is even worse than I imagined. Plum has practically thrown a party to celebrate her discovery of the Wakefield Hall etiquette guide. Almost all the common-

14

room chairs have been arranged in two half-moon rows, and the chairs are full of girls. Their backs are to me; they're all facing the cleared area, the open space in the center, where the last chair is placed. As if it's on a stage.

And Plum's performing. She's sitting on the chair, knees squeezed tightly together, feet in the air, halfway through copying the large black-and-white photo in the guide, which she's holding in one hand, high up and facing out, so that everyone in the room can see it as clearly as possible.

It's me, in the terrible, stomach-turning "How to Exit a Car with Grace and Dignity" section.

Plum turns her head and spots me standing there. I have to give the cow some credit for her nerve; she doesn't look at all taken aback at having the object of her mockery walk in halfway through her act.

"Scarlett! How *fortuitous!*" she exclaims, dropping her feet to the ground, her heavily mascara'd green eyes opening even wider. "I mean, you're the *expert* on this whole etiquette subject, aren't you? Come over here, will you, and show me how to keep my legs together? It's something I seem to have a little problem with from time to time, but I'm sure it isn't an issue for *you!*"

Sycophantic titters greet this latest sally. Everyone turns to look at me, craning their necks over the backs of their chairs. And I realize with horror that it's happening all over again.

Plum and I were at St. Tabby's together, up till last summer, when I was asked to leave because of all the media attention surrounding Dan McAndrew's death. I was just another insignificant student who did gymnastics after school almost every day and stayed well away from the ruling clique of girls, because any attention they gave me would definitely be negative.

While Princess Plum—beautiful, rich, and socially from the top drawer—was the supreme ruler of all she surveyed. She was so influential that girls copied her slavishly, hoping to win her approval and avoid being on the receiving end of her sharp tongue.

But St. Tabby's was one of the smartest, most socially important girls' schools in England. When Plum got expelled and sent here instead, I really hoped that her particular brand of mean-girl nastiness wouldn't work as well at Wakefield Hall, where brains are valued much more highly than the number of times you've been in *Tatler* that year.

Clearly, I was wrong.

Because every single head turned to me looks like an amateur version of Plum.

Plum's hair is pulled loosely up on her head with an elastic; all the girls with long-enough hair to imitate her are wearing theirs in a similar style. Their eyelashes are mascara'd just like Plum's, their lips glossed like hers. Now that I get a good look at the room, I can see that Plum's lounging outfit of skinny-fit T-shirt, flannel pajama bottoms, and furry slippers has been reproduced, as closely as possible, on every girl present. Her wrists are encircled with bracelets made of big silvered glass beads, which she's been wearing nonstop since she came back from the Christmas holidays, and most of the other girls have tried to copy them, buying versions as close to Plum's originals as they can, but, of course, not quite succeeding.

In the space of just a few weeks, Plum has managed to create a whole new army of Plum-bots.

Complete with matching jewelry.

The only person who hasn't succumbed to Plum's brain-washing is Taylor, who promised me that she'd stand quietly by my side during this confrontation, unless I gave her the signal to use her amazing intimidation skills. Although when I glance at Taylor, who is standing with her arms crossed over her chest and grimacing at Plum as though she'd strangled Taylor's dog, I realize she doesn't have to say anything in order to put the fear of God into someone. Taylor is, quite frankly, toughness personified.

Which is why I'm grateful that she's in my corner.

"Give me that," I say, marching round the rows of chairs, advancing on Plum and snatching the etiquette guide out of her hand.

"But, Scarlett!" Plum mimes shock, one hand to her mouth. "You can't take that away. Without it, how will we all learn to be properly behaved young ladies?"

"It'd take more than an etiquette guide to teach you that," I snap.

Plum's eyes narrow into slits.

"You were nothing at St. Tabby's," she hisses. "*Nothing.* And then you got invited to one party—one!—and a couple of boys noticed you, mainly because you were just *fresh meat,* and you got your head swelled almost as much as your ridiculous, fake-looking boobs!"

There are gasps from the rows of spectators at this round of insults. All the girls are leaning forward as if they were at the circus and we were doing life-threatening stunts.

"Oh, just go and buy yourself a Wonderbra," I cut in. "Honestly, it's tragic how obsessed you are with my boobs.

Maybe if you didn't starve yourself you'd have some of your own!"

More gasps. Plum tosses back her head theatrically and glares at me.

"I do *not* starve myself," she barks.

"No, you've got other ways to keep skinny, don't you?" I snap back. "Ways that don't work for poor people, right?"

Lizzie Livermore, sitting in the front row, claps her hands over her mouth in shock that I've brought this up. Lizzie has always been a Plum-bot, even before Plum landed at Wakefield Hall. Insecure, fashion-obsessed, and very, very rich, Lizzie hangs out with Plum and her clique in London, buying her entrance to their smart party set by using the credit cards her father gives her instead of the attention she really wants from him.

Ever since Plum arrived here, Lizzie's run around after her like a yappy little dog. And Lizzie knows exactly what I'm referring to, the reason Plum had to leave St. Tabby's. Plum's best frenemy, Nadia Farouk, posted a video clip on YouTube of Plum snorting coke and saying that "dieting is for poor people."

I may have gone too far, however. Plum practically hisses like a snake at this.

"At least I haven't *killed* anyone!" she says furiously, pointing one manicured finger at me.

But I can tell from the malign expression on her face what she's about to spit out, and as soon as she opens her mouth I'm saying equally loudly, covering her words:

"Outside! *Now!*"

I can see that no one expects Plum to obey. There are more gasps of surprise as, reluctantly, she pushes back the chair and stands up.

Damn. I'm in trainers, and Plum towers over me. It was a lot easier to face off against her when she was sitting down. No girl who isn't as tall and slim as Plum herself would be comfortable in her skin standing next to Plum. I feel as squat and stumpy as a pillar. In the dark glass of the window behind us I see our reflections, and I wince at the comparison.

I can't compete with her in looks, either. I'm pretty enough—with my dark wavy hair, blue eyes, and pale skin, I'm a dead ringer for the Wakefield women in most of the family portraits. But Plum's photogenic, chiseled cheekbones, perfect straight nose, and mesmerizing green eyes put her way beyond mere pretty, securely into the "beautiful" category.

I really don't want to be standing next to her with everyone else gaping at us. I swivel and walk quickly past the rows of girls, heading for the door. Though I double-take briefly as, acknowledging Lizzie with a swift nod, I see who's sitting next to her: a girl called Susan, who's in my Latin class. Tall, blond, and willowy, Susan is one of the prettiest girls in school, but has always been shy and seemingly uninterested in her appearance. Now, with her white-blond hair pulled back from her face, her thick lashes mascara'd and her near-invisible eyebrows penciled to light brown, she's a total knockout.

She could give Plum a run for her money in the beauty stakes, I think savagely. *Hope Plum doesn't destroy her for it.*

"Want me to come with you?" Taylor asks.

I shake my head. "Just keep an eye on everyone else, okay?"

Taylor nods in agreement, then scans the group for any interlopers who might want to follow Plum and me outside.

I stalk out into the corridor and down to the far end, by the fire door, an isolated spot where no one can sneak up on us and eavesdrop. Plum walks as haughtily down the corridor in her fluffy slippers as if she were strutting down a Milan catwalk. Behind her, Taylor exits the room and leans against the wall, making sure that everyone else stays inside the common room.

"Wherever did you find such a butch bodyguard, Scarlett?" Plum says sarcastically.

I have to admit, Plum has nailed Taylor's posture. Taylor is wide-shouldered from all the pull-ups she does, and her equally muscly arms are folded across her chest. She could easily pass for a bouncer if she shaved off the shaggy dark hair that's falling into her eyes. Plum made the comment loudly enough for Taylor to hear, and I see Taylor's thick dark brows pull together in annoyance; though she's resolutely nongirly, she hates it when people comment on her looking mannish.

That's the trouble with Plum. She's incredibly talented at homing in on people's weaknesses, inserting the knife tip to test for flinching, and then twisting it deep. The best thing to do is ignore these comments, but right now I don't have the mental fortitude to remind myself of that.

"You crossed the line," I snarl.

"Ooh! Dramatic! What are you going to do?" Plum retorts. "Go running to your grandmummy?"

I've got no choice but to call her bluff.

"Sure," I say immediately. "I'll go and wake her up right

20

now. Do you want to come along with me, or wait till tomorrow to get your trust fund access frozen?"

Plum narrows her eyes at me. "You *bitch*."

She takes a step toward me, her fists clenched.

"Pot, meet kettle," I say coldly, staring up into Plum's eyes, not flinching for a second. Plum may be a lot taller than me, but she's just a skinny minny. After all my years of gymnastics and now my workouts with Taylor, I'm much, much stronger than my curvy physique suggests.

I could take Plum in a fight with one arm tied behind my back. I've already had a physical encounter with her once, at St. Tabby's, and I won that very easily. I glare back at her, telling her with my eyes and my posture not to put her hands on me. I see that she's reading the message loud and clear.

"This is far from over," she says angrily, turning on her heel. "Get out of my way," she snaps at Taylor as she advances, raising her hand, bracelets jangling, to push back a stray lock of her hair. Taylor actually steps aside for her almost deferentially, which surprises me. Plum is acting like a princess, but I didn't expect Taylor, of all people, to obey her haughty commands.

And just as Plum sweeps majestically past Taylor, she throws over her shoulder at me: "I'm going to find more copies of that etiquette guide and make you a total laughingstock with the entire school. I've got nothing else to do in this bloody boring hellhole but make your life a misery, Scarlett Wakefield!"

Oh God. Nowadays all I seem to do is put out one fire after another. I shiver. Because I know that cow means every word she says.

21

Three

A ROCK AND A HARD PLACE

"What did you mean about her trust fund?" Taylor asks as we walk back down the staircase of the Pankhurst dormitory.

I look quickly at my watch: ten minutes till curfew. Just enough time to fill her in.

"I promised my grandmother not to tell," I say. "But now it's all blowing up, it's stupid for you not to know."

"*Anything* to do with Plum, I ought to know," Taylor says immediately. "Information is power."

I nod. She's absolutely right.

So I tell her what happened in my grandmother's study a few weeks ago, when Plum arrived at Wakefield Hall.

. . .

Being summoned to see my grandmother is always a nerve-racking experience. Even when she wasn't the head-mistress of the school I attended, she was extremely intimi-dating. Now it's a double whammy. Whether I've done something wrong as a granddaughter or as a pupil, it's Lady

Wakefield (which she insists I call her during term time) I have to answer to.

And somehow, whenever I get a message telling me I have to go to see my grandmother, I always assume that it's because I've done something wrong.

This time, however, was unprecedented. Someone had certainly done something wrong, but, for a blissful change, it wasn't me.

Plum was sitting opposite my grandmother, a scowl on her face, every inch of her body expressing an overpowering wish to be as far away as possible. The weird thing was that I actually felt a rush of sympathy for her. She looked exactly how I felt every time I was in my grandmother's presence. For once, Plum and I had something in common.

"Scarlett, I have taken the unusual step of calling you in," my grandmother said, her enunciation, as always, exquisite. "This matter directly concerns you, as you may imagine. Please sit down."

I pulled up a straight-backed chair and obeyed, crossing my legs at the knee and folding my hands in my lap, the way Lady Wakefield considers proper for well-brought-up young ladies.

"Plum, sit up properly like Scarlett is doing," my grandmother said firmly. "I take it you were never taught deportment at St. Tabitha's?"

"No, we weren't," Plum said sullenly, sitting up and shooting me a nasty glare.

"No, we weren't, *Lady Wakefield*," my grandmother corrected her. "We are strict about manners here at Wakefield Hall, as you will find."

I couldn't help but be proud of my grandmother, the way she was effortlessly turning Princess Plum, who had teachers at St. Tabby's jumping to obey her whims, into a sulky sixteen-year-old girl being told off for slouching. With her sleek silver hair, her bright blue eyes, and her perfectly chosen twinset and pearls, my grandmother, sitting behind her desk with absolute authority, was making it more than clear who was in charge. I had to admit that it was strangely comforting.

"Scarlett," she continued, "I have agreed to take Miss Saybourne here as a student at Wakefield Hall under certain strict conditions. Some of those, naturally, considering the circumstances under which Miss Saybourne was asked to leave St. Tabitha's, involve restrictions on her personal conduct agreed upon by herself and her parents, and do not concern you."

In other words, Plum was under lockdown to make sure she didn't get her hands on any illicit substances or corrupt anyone else's morals. I wondered before why my grandmother had agreed to take Plum on as a pupil; she must have found the whole YouTube video scandal incredibly shocking. But looking at her then, at the severity with which she was regarding Plum, I realized in a flash of revelation what her motivation was for admitting wild-child Plum to the highly respectable confines of Wakefield Hall.

My grandmother really loves a challenge.

"*But*," she went on, "it would be foolish to ignore the fact that you and Plum were together at St. Tabitha's when the unfortunate incident occurred with that poor young man."

This was such a magnificently understated way to refer to Dan's death that Plum turned her head to stare at me incredulously, as if saying, *Did you hear what she just said?* And I raised my eyebrows fractionally, acknowledging her in an equally silent reply, *Yes, this is Lady Wakefield in action. Scary, eh?*

Plum and I were actually on the same side for a fleeting moment. Wow. Double weirdness.

"Plum has given her word that she will neither refer to that incident in general, nor associate your name with it in particular," my grandmother proceeded elegantly.

My eyebrows shot up as far as they could go. *Right. Plum's "given her word."* I remembered a story I read about a Hollywood producer who constantly misspoke and once said a verbal contract wasn't worth the paper it was written on. Well, as far as I was concerned, *Plum* and *verbal contracts* shouldn't ever exist in the same sentence.

But Lady Wakefield was far ahead of me.

"This undertaking," she added, staring hard at Plum, "consists of a formal document signed by her and her parents, as she is legally a minor. They have agreed, as a condition of my accepting Plum as a student, that should she break this oath in any way, they will immediately block her access to her income from her trust fund, which is under their control."

It was all I could do not to whistle aloud with appreciation for my grandmother's genius. It was a simple and brilliant scheme to deter Plum from opening her mouth about my involvement in Dan's death.

And from the way Plum's lips were pressed tightly together, the scheme was obviously working.

"You may leave us now, Plum," my grandmother said. "I would like to speak to Scarlett in private. I hope you will be very happy at Wakefield Hall. You have a very good academic record, and I'm sure you will find the intellectual atmosphere here stimulating enough to fully occupy your time."

As Plum pushed back her chair and stood up, my grandmother's bright blue eyes went straight to the hem of Plum's skirt, which had ridden up while she was sitting, and without a word being said, Plum obediently reached down to tug her hemline back toward her knees.

That was fantastic entertainment. What wasn't so much fun was the killer glare Plum shot me as she turned to leave the room, which indicated all too clearly that I'd pay for having seen her kowtow to my grandmother.

As the door closed behind her, I let out a breath I hadn't even realized I was holding. I felt a rush of relief, because my grandmother had made sure I was protected. I'd been freaking out ever since I saw Plum arrive at school in a cloud of fur and cigarette smoke, surrounded by piles of Louis Vuitton suitcases. When Dan died, the papers couldn't report my name because I was a minor, so they gave me a nickname: the Kiss of Death Girl. The last thing I wanted was that awful nickname to follow me to Wakefield Hall. Because she hung out with Plum and her set, Lizzie knew my story, but Lizzie is easily intimidated, and she was much too terrified of my grandmother's wrath to breathe a word.

Plum was a much tougher nut. It had taken the threat of

no more money to spend on furs and Vuitton to ensure that her lips were sealed.

"*Thank* you," I said to my grandmother, with such fervency that she smiled. Not the usual small, wintry curve of her lips while her eyes stayed cool and clear, but a rare, affectionate smile that deepened her crow's-feet and the creases on either side of her mouth.

"Parents send their daughters to Wakefield Hall for the best education possible, and to perfect their manners and social skills," she said dryly. "*Not* to waste their time on lurid scandal-mongering."

Decoded, that meant "You're welcome."

My grandmother propped her hands on the desk in front of her and steepled her fingers. "Scarlett, I asked you to stay behind because it was perfectly obvious that there isn't the best of blood between you and young Miss Saybourne. As far as I'm concerned, the unpleasant little episode that caused her to be expelled from St. Tabitha's is now in the past. She has promised to turn over a new leaf, and her parents assure me that she will."

Right, I thought. *And after that she'll sprout wings and fly away.*

"So what I said to her applies to you as well," she concluded. "Miss Saybourne has brought disgrace on her very old and well-respected county family by her actions, and she should be thoroughly ashamed of herself. But her parents, the headmistress of St. Tabitha's, and I have already taken care of reprimanding her. I don't want anyone at Wakefield Hall to rub salt in her wounds. Particularly not you."

I nodded dutifully. I was more involved in the video of

Plum being posted on the Web than my grandmother or Plum know; I've done enough to bring Plum down.

"I have protected you, Scarlett, because that incident with the boy last year was in no way your fault," she said. "But let me make this very clear: Wakefield Hall is your home, as well as your school. That puts the onus firmly on you to behave better than any other student. You are not just any sixth-former. You are the eventual chatelaine of the Hall, and I expect you to conduct yourself accordingly. If I hear of any fights or feuding between you and Miss Saybourne, I will hold you directly responsible."

She adjusted her pearls, shot me a direct, piercingly blue stare, and lowered her head to the leather blotter on her desk.

"That is all," she said, uncapping her fountain pen.

*   *   *

Taylor's eyes widen with shock. "Oh, jeez, you are *so fricking . . .*"

"I know," I say gloomily. "I'm totally and utterly shafted."

"That," Taylor says, smirking, "is *exactly* the word I was looking for."

"I was just planning to stay out of her way as much as possible," I say.

Taylor's smirk widens into one of those awkward grins that mean you know you shouldn't find something funny, but you just can't help it.

"Well, *that* plan worked out really well tonight," she comments. "Maybe I shouldn't have told you what she was up to."

"No, you did the right thing." I shiver at the memory of Plum imitating me getting out of a car. "But that's the trouble. If I stay out of her way, she makes fun of me behind my back, and if I take her on, we have a psycho confrontation."

"I think that's called being between a rock and a hard place," Taylor says.

"Welcome to my world," I sigh.

four
AQUAMARINE

Thank goodness, the next day is Sunday, which means it's relatively easy to stay out of Plum's way. For once, I'm actually grateful that I don't live in one of the dormitory wings. When I started at Wakefield Hall as a pupil, my grandmother decreed that I should stay full-time at my aunt Gwen's cottage, where I already had a room for the school holidays. Aunt Gwen's always pretty much loathed me, and it seems only polite to reciprocate, so it's never been an ideal arrangement.

But now, at least, it does mean that I have a Plum-free zone. And one thing Aunt Gwen never does is bother me; her policy has always been to pretend, as best as possible, that I'm not there at all.

In the morning she's out at church, so I make myself breakfast and finish my English essay. Taylor and I go for a run and workout at lunchtime, and by three p.m. I'm showered, dressed, and leaving the cottage without even a "See you later" to Aunt Gwen, who's watching a Miss Marple mystery on TV in the living room. I used to feel I ought to say hello and goodbye when I came in or went out, but you feel pretty idiotic greeting someone who never answers you, so eventually I just gave up.

My heart's beating faster as I walk up the drive toward school. This is what really matters. This is what my whole day's been leading toward. These are the times I feel wholly and completely alive.

Because I'm on my way to meet Jase.

I crunch onto the drive. To my right is the main part of Wakefield Hall, an imposing, turreted building of ivy-covered gray stone, with a big stained-glass window curving over the huge iron-studded door. Wakefield has been in the family for so many generations I can't count them out without the help of the family tree. And as my father's daughter, I'm the heir to all this. Everything I survey will be mine one day.

It's a feeling that always makes me shiver with a mixture of pride and fear of the responsibility. And thinking of my father, I have one of the flashes of memory that flood into my mind every so often—an image of my parents, who died when I was four years old. My father picking me up and sliding me down the banister of the great staircase in the Hall, the polished wood shining, the smell of beeswax suddenly in my nostrils. Pretending he's going to let go his grip on me, making me squeal with a mixture of fear and excitement in which the latter definitely predominated.

And my mother, standing by the newel post, arms out to catch me as I slide toward her, laughing. The huge front door open behind her, the sun pouring in, haloing her light brown hair around her face, turning the strands to gold.

31

Most of all, I remember the trust I had in my father, the absolute confidence that he would keep me safe.

It can't have been more than six months later that they died.

I swallow very hard to get down the big lump in my throat. It's as difficult as trying to get a whole cherry past my tonsils. No matter how many times I tell myself bravely that having a father like Mr. Barnes is worse than having no parents at all, it's never quite as reassuring as I believe it will be.

Don't think about it any more, Scarlett, I tell myself firmly. *Think about Jase. Think about the future, not the past.*

I'm dressed for a winter afternoon out on a motorbike—jeans, a wool sweater, a leather jacket, boots with a one-inch heel. But the jeans are nice and tight, to show off my legs; the sweater is turquoise, to show off my blue eyes; and the jacket, bought with my Christmas money, is soft as butter and a shade of really dark blue that I agonized over for ages. I wasn't sure if it was cool enough. Would black be safer? But wasn't that a bit boring? When I eventually bought the jacket and wore it at school this term, I caught Plum giving it a distinctly envious glance, which was all the confirmation I needed that I'd made the right decision.

God, shopping is *hard.* Even when you're lucky enough to have a trust fund, plus a grandmother who throws money at you for Christmas and birthdays because she hasn't the faintest idea what to buy you.

I don't get any presents from Aunt Gwen, but then I don't get anything for Aunt Gwen either. It's been like that as long as I can remember, a mutual admission that we really don't know each other's tastes and, to be honest, don't have any interest in finding them out. Although Aunt Gwen dislikes me intensely, I must admit that I can't completely blame her. My grandmother, after all, makes her live in the gatehouse cottage, which is pretty tiny, and always refers to me as the heir to Wakefield, even though my aunt is her daughter. I mean, my father was her son, so Aunt Gwen and I should share it, right?

I do mean to talk to my grandmother about this someday. But I'm much too intimidated to do it now. Especially what with having to call her Lady Wakefield during term time . . .

I'm through the courtyard and rounding the side of the new school wing, running down the narrow passage that's technically off-limits for students, because it leads to the staff cottages. As I emerge from the narrow lane, Jase, who's leaning against his bike, a helmet dangling from each hand, flashes me the broadest of grins. There's no pretense at being cool, that he isn't happy to see me, that he hasn't been waiting for me. It's my favorite thing about Jase: he never plays that kind of game.

Well, that and the fact that he's completely gorgeous, of course. I never said I wasn't shallow.

"You took your time," he says, his bright gold eyes glinting with amusement.

"Taylor and I went for a really long run," I say apologetically. "She's worse than a personal trainer, she shouts and shouts if I even think about stopping."

Jase cracks a grin.

"Fair dos," he says. "I wouldn't want Taylor shouting at me. She's got shoulders like a brickie."

"She made us do tons of push-ups too," I boast.

"Let's have a feel, then." Jase reaches out to squeeze my bicep. "Hey, not bad for a girl."

He pulls me closer.

"Give me a kiss to show you're sorry," he says teasingly. "Don't worry, my dad's off at the pub. He won't be back till late."

Blushing in anticipation, I go up on tiptoe and plant a soft, slow kiss on his lips. My eyes close. They always close of their own accord when I kiss him. Sometimes I try to keep them open, just to see if I can. But the experience of being that near to Jase, feeling his warmth, smelling his skin, touching him so intimately, is so overpowering that I never manage it.

His arms wrap around me reflexively as he starts to kiss me back, his full lips nipping at mine, the tip of his tongue touching my lower lip, easing my mouth open, a shiver running through me as I meet his tongue with mine.

And then the two motorcycle helmets clang together behind my back, and we both jump.

"Whoops! Forgot I was holding 'em," Jase says, pulling back. He winks at me. "You shouldn't get me all distracted like that."

"Hey, it's not *my* fault." I make a face at him and take my helmet. "You're the one who told me to kiss you."

We put our helmets on and climb onto the bike. Jase revs it up. And it's the oddest thing, because the helmet really restricts how much vision you have. But out of the corner of my eye, I think I see movement, and nervously, just in case Jase is mistaken and his dad isn't safely off at the pub after all, I turn my head to check out what it is.

34

There's an old lady standing in the window of the Barneses' cottage. White hair pulled up on top of her head in a sparse little bun. Round wire-framed glasses, pink wrinkled cheeks, her hands resting in front of her on what looks like a cane. The curtains at the window are faded lace, pulled back with ties, and they frame her so neatly that the whole image looks like a sentimental picture, too cozy to be true.

I think of my own grandmother, with her sleek white bob of hair, her smart tweeds and twinsets, her bright blue eyes that don't need any help to see clearly, with 20/20 vision. Nothing cozy about her at all. They might both be little old ladies, but that seems to be all they have in common, Jase's grandmother and mine.

And then the bike takes off, gravel spurting from beneath its wheels, my body thudding against Jase's back as I cling to him tightly. All I can think about is the sheer joy of motion. I'll never tire of being on the bike with Jase, never. Speed, excitement, having my body pressed so closely against his, feeling his chest rise and fall under my gloved hands.

I just wish we didn't have to wear helmets. I hate not being able to cuddle my head into his neck when we're out on the bike.

• • •

"Your cheeks are all pink." Jase reaches across the table to stroke my face. "Look at you."

I mutter something about lifting the visor to get the wind in my face, but honestly I think that the reason I'm flushed is that even after a couple of months of going out with Jase, I

35

still get a bit overcome by how gorgeous he is. I can't quite take it for granted yet. When we walked into this little coffee shop together, I was sure that everyone was looking up and asking themselves what on earth a boy this good-looking was doing with me.

He's lounging on his side of the coffee-shop booth, his back against the wall, his legs stretched out in front of him, one knee up, looking so sexy in his leather bike trousers with their dark red stripes it's no wonder I'm blushing. The feel of his hand on my cheek, warm and caressing, is so lovely I want to turn my head into his palm and start purring like a cat.

However, Jase must be having much less happy thoughts than I am, because when he speaks again, his voice is deep and serious.

"I hate all this sneaking around." His hand moves through my hair, playing with the curls; then he leans forward to twist one of them around his finger. "I wish we could just hang out normally, you know? Have you meet my mates, go to the normal places we all go, in Wakefield, not have to ride for miles and miles to find some coffee shop in a buried-alive village my dad would never come to."

"I know," I sigh, taking his hand and twining my fingers through his. "Though I do like the long rides on the bike."

He smiles at me, his teeth impossibly white against his golden-brown skin.

"Yeah, but we end up wasting a lot of time together," he says, tightening his fingers on mine. "I know all that star-crossed-lovers stuff sounds cool when it's in *Romeo and Juliet*, but in real life, if you ask me, it's well overrated."

I gape at him.

"What?" Heightened color tinges his cheeks, despite the even tone of his skin. "You think just because I didn't go to a private school I don't know anything about posh writers? We did *Romeo and Juliet* in English last year."

Actually, it was his referring to us as lovers that caused my mouth to dry up temporarily, but I'm not going to tell him that.

"No, I didn't mean that, Jase." I squeeze his hand. "I'm just . . . I really liked what you said."

"Well, it's true." Jase rolls his eyes. "I mean, it looks great on TV, or in a film, you know? Feuding families, you can't be together, all that stuff, it's really romantic. But it always ends up going wrong. Someone dies, or goes to prison, or something. It never ends up with the two of them being able to be boyfriend and girlfriend properly, with their parents or whatever apologizing and saying they were wrong. I'm pretty sick of this, Scarlett."

One of the things I like most about Jase is that he's so direct. He isn't the kind of boy who enjoys the drama and intrigue of sneaking around. He just wants to have a normal boyfriend/girlfriend relationship—

Oh my God. He just said boyfriend *and* girlfriend *for the first time ever.*

And lovers.

Oh my God.

I'm still registering that he's used all those magic words when it dawns on me how dark his tone of voice is.

"You're sick of it? Does that mean you're breaking up with me?" I blurt out in total panic.

"Jesus, Scarlett." He pulls his hand away and runs it over

his tight dark curls, and for a moment I think I'll burst into tears. His eyes darken to a deep bronze as he stares at me, frowning. "No, I don't want to break up, you idiot. I just want to be able to go out like normal teenagers do without worrying that my dad's going to catch us and throw a huge wobbly. Like last night, or that time at the lake."

I shudder as I remember Mr. Barnes catching Jase and me together at the Wakefield Hall private lake. All we were doing was climbing trees—I was balancing on a branch, showing off my gymnastics skills for Jase. His dad went after me, and he and Jase came to blows. Then his dad warned me and Jase to stay away from each other, very menacingly.

What neither of us really understands is *why*. Why does his dad mind so much that Jase and I are seeing each other? It seems crazy to think it's some kind of weird feudal objection to the son of the gardener going out with the daughter of the house, especially since you'd think it'd be my grandmother who'd be making a fuss about that kind of thing, rather than Jase's dad.

It's a complete mystery to both of us. But his father was so scarily, violently angry that neither of us wants to face a scene like that ever again if we can possibly avoid it.

I'm so lost in my speculations about Jase's dad and his inexplicably horrible attitude to us that Jase has to clear his throat very loudly to get my attention. When I finally do pull my head out of the clouds and focus on him, I see that he's frowning grumpily.

"What is it?" I ask, just as he shoves his hand across the table, deposits a small wooden box in front of me and slides his hand back again, putting it in his lap, as if he doesn't want to be held responsible for what he just did. He's still frowning.

"Jase?"

I open the box, and gasp. Inside is a pendant on a fine silver chain. It's a silver circle, with a blue stone fixed in a silver setting to the top of the circle, the whole thing about an inch and a half in diameter. The stone is an aquamarine, the same color as my eyes. I pick up the pendant by the chain and it dangles in the air, the stone catching the light and glittering brightly, the color of the Mediterranean Sea a little out from the coast, before it darkens to the depths of the ocean: a bright, clear, beautiful blue.

I can't speak. I just stare at it for what feels like hours. And then I lift my head to look at Jase, my whole heart in my eyes.

"It was my mum's," he says gruffly. "She never took it with her when she left. I dunno why. I found it in her room. I thought for ages she'd come back for it, but she never did."

Jase's mum walked out on him and his dad when he was young. It's pretty sad. She doesn't even live that far away, just a few villages over, but he barely ever sees her.

"My gran threw out all Mum's things after a while, but I kept a couple of 'em, just to remind me of her," Jase says. "Hid 'em in my room, because Gran would've chucked 'em out if she'd found 'em. I was going through it all the other day, and this really made me think of you."

I know now why he's frowning: it's hard for him to talk about his mum at the best of times. And this is even harder, because it's giving up a dream he had: that she'd come back to see the son she left behind.

"I hope you don't mind that it's sort of secondhand," he says, looking at me intently, trying to read my reaction. "But it's so perfect for you—your eyes, it's just the same color."

"Aquamarine," I say, smiling at him, trying very hard not to cry at the same time. "It's an aquamarine."

"Do you like it?" His bright eyes are worried now. "I was going to give it to you for Christmas, but we hadn't been . . . I mean, we weren't, you know . . ." He clears his throat again.

I know exactly what he means. I agonized for ages about whether I should give him a Christmas present too, but I wasn't sure what our status was, and I was terrified of putting him off by making him think I was too keen. Also, what I really wanted to give him was a pair of Ducati motorcycle gloves I'd seen in a Sunday magazine, which I knew he would love, but they cost a fortune. Not a problem for me with my trust fund, but it might have been overwhelming for Jase, reminding him of the huge differential between his spending power and mine.

We just exchanged cards in the end, and then Jase went off on Boxing Day, straight after Christmas, on a fortnight-long skiing trip he'd had planned with friends for months, so I had plenty of time on my own to mope around, bored and restless, with Taylor off in the U.S. on holiday with her family. I was nervous that Jase might meet someone else skiing in France, some gorgeous French girl with the sexy bedroom eyes and unwashed hair all French girls seemed to have in films, but he rang me as soon as he got back. For the past three weeks we've been seeing more and more of each other.

"And then I was going to wait for Valentine's Day, but I

just couldn't hold out any longer," he confesses, blushing a little. "Every time I saw you, I wanted to give it to you. Oh, no, Scarlett, don't cry. *Jesus*."

"Who's the cappuccino for, then?" the waitress says brightly, setting the tray down on the table. "Oh, what a pretty necklace! Aren't you a lucky girl?"

I nod violently, completely incapable of speech.

"The cappuccino's for her." Jase looks absolutely panic-stricken at the prospect of my breaking into tears and blubbing all over the waitress. I manage a sort of laugh, because his expression's so funny, but it comes out as a gulp, and the waitress smiles understandingly as she puts the cappuccino down in front of me.

"So the caffe latte must be for your boyfriend," she says, sliding it over to him. "There you go, dear. And two slices of chocolate cake."

The chocolate cake looks amazing. Three layers, each sandwiched with thick, rich chocolate icing, and a generous dollop of whipped cream on top.

"I love it," I finally manage to say to Jase, looking back down as the waitress retreats.

"It does look really good," he agrees.

"No!" I'm grinning now. "The necklace, you idiot, not the cake!"

He's grinning back, his golden eyes shining.

"Hey, if you're going to call me an idiot, I'll have to take that back."

He makes a playful grab for the box, but I whisk it out of his reach.

"No way. It wouldn't look as good on you," I point out.

He looks wistful.

"Aren't you going to put it on?" he asks.

"Cake first," I say, suddenly craving sugar and coffee and chocolate to distract me from the rush of powerful emotions surging through me.

Also, I know that if I put on the necklace and look at myself I really will burst into tears, and there's no way Jase or I want that to happen in the middle of Ye Olde Coffee Shoppe. I think he gets what I'm trying to communicate, because he nods and reaches for his coffee cup.

The cake is absolutely delicious, even better than it looks, and the sugar hits the spot so successfully that I forget to be ladylike and not stuff my face in front of a boy. Instead, I shovel it in like a steam train driver heaving coal into the engine, so fast and furiously that I don't immediately notice that Jase isn't eating. It's only when I look up, my mouth unattractively full, that I realize he's frozen with his fork halfway on its way to the plate.

"Whaa?" I say, my mouth glued up with the icing.

He nods sharply to my right shoulder. Still chewing, I swivel around.

My aunt Gwen's standing there, just behind the side of the booth.

And she's glaring so hard at both of us it looks as if her eyes are going to pop out of their sockets.

five
CUTTING OUR LOSSES

Aunt Gwen is *not* an attractive woman. I often speculate that one of the reasons my grandmother doesn't treat her as well as she might is that unlike me, Aunt Gwen doesn't have the classic Wakefield looks. She's sandy in coloring, with pale to nonexistent eyebrows and lashes, and sparse, frizzy ginger hair. Her skin is blotchy and red—her bathroom's full of lotions and homeopathic remedies, none of which seems to make the slightest difference—and though her eyes are blue, they're not the bright Wakefield aquamarine, but so watery and washed-out they're almost colorless.

But the worst part of Aunt Gwen's appearance, unfortunately, is the way her eyes bulge out like gobstoppers. She has a medical condition that makes her eyeballs protrude from their sockets; the younger girls at school call her Miss Froggy. And whenever she gets cross, her eyes bug out even farther. When I was little, one of my recurring nightmares was that Aunt Gwen would get so angry with me that her eyeballs would actually pop out from their sockets and drop, squashily, onto the floor.

Right now, they're bulging out so far that I immediately revert to my childhood state and stare at them in terror, willing them to stay where they are.

"*Scarlett!*" she says furiously. "What are you doing?"

I swallow my cake and take a deep breath, letting it go down so I don't choke, taking the time to swiftly review the school rules in my mind: no, I honestly can't think of a single one I'm breaking by being out on a Sunday afternoon in a tea shop with Jase. So why on earth is she acting like this?

"I'm having a coffee," I say eventually, feeling my brow furrow in puzzlement at her attitude. "With a friend, on *Sunday*, when I'm allowed to leave school from ten to seven. That's the rule, isn't it?"

Jase, hearing my voice sharpening, gives me a kick under the table to tell me to cool it.

"And who is this *friend?*" she demands, staring at Jase. Though I'm sure she knows the answer already.

"This is Jase Barnes, Aunt Gwen," I say, unable to keep the impatience out of my voice. "You must've seen him around the grounds tons of times. He's Mr. Barnes's son, he does a lot of the gardening and—"

"And who gave you permission to come out with him?" she interrupts.

I don't know what's going on, but this is way over the line.

"I don't *need* permission," I snap, and this time when Jase kicks me, I kick him right back. "Believe me, I know what the rules are for sixth-formers, okay? I can go out with my friends on weekday afternoons and on Sundays, and I only need to check with a member of staff if I'm going beyond Wakefield or the surrounding villages."

Of course, this rule was actually made to avoid sixth-formers' having to clear it with their form teacher every time they're taken out to lunch by their families. But what Jase and I are doing is totally covered by the letter of the law, if maybe not the spirit.

I can see Aunt Gwen knows I'm right by the frustrated expression on her face. She looks past me now, at Jase. She's like a monster in a horror film turning, slowly, to survey its prey, her buggy, washed-out eyes swelling as if they're going to completely take over her face.

"Does your father know you're out with Scarlett, young man?" she says nastily.

Jase's eyes widen at the question, and though he opens his mouth to speak, no words emerge.

"I knew it!" Aunt Gwen says triumphantly. "I *knew* your father wouldn't approve of this!"

"Excuse me, Aunt Gwen," I break in frantically, seeing Jase cowering nervously under her attack, "but this is *so* not your business! I'm allowed to be out, and Jase is eighteen, which means he's an adult and doesn't have to ask anyone's permission to do anything. You're making an awful scene about nothing at all."

I fix Jase with a stare, silently imploring him to be strong, not to back down just because Aunt Gwen is a Wakefield. It's horribly clear to me that if we don't stand our ground now, we'll be in real trouble trying to see each other in the future.

"We're in a *coffee shop*, for goodness' sake," I continue,

getting crosser and crosser by the second. "We're eating *cake*. I mean, if you'd caught us getting drunk and messing around behind Wakefield village cricket pavilion . . ."

Jase stares at me in surprise. How sheltered does he think I am? I mean, everyone knows where the wilder kids in the village hang out!

" . . . then yeah, you could have a go at us. But *this*?" I gesture around Ye Olde Coffee Shoppe, with its ornamental brasses hung on the walls, its gingham curtains and white lace doilies on the cake stands. "I'd have thought you'd be *thankful* this is where I come with my boyfriend," I finish.

It must be the use of the word *boyfriend* that sends her into overdrive. The next thing I know, her hand is gripping my arm, tight as a vise, digging into my skin so sharply that I find myself rising in my seat to ease the pain of her fingers.

"Ow!" I yell.

"You're coming back to school with me *right now*," Aunt Gwen hisses, a bubble of saliva collecting in the side of her mouth.

"I will not! I don't have to be back till seven."

Aunt Gwen might have a surprisingly powerful grip for a geography and math teacher, but if there's one thing gymnastics gives you, it's strong hands—all that landing on them and swinging off bars. I grab her wrist with my other hand and wrench it off my arm so violently that she staggers back. Sometimes, I actually don't know my own strength.

"Scarlett," Jase says quickly as I start to sit down in the booth again. "Go back with her. It's not worth it."

My heart thuds. He's giving in. "You don't mean that. I'm *allowed* to be out with you."

Aunt Gwen, slinging the strap of her handbag over her shoulder, approaches us again, a martial light in her horrible eyes.

"Seriously. She won't leave us in peace now anyway. We might as well cut our losses," he says resignedly.

Our hands meet across the table, mine clinging to his.

"This is *mad*," I say miserably.

"I know." He squeezes my hand tight. "I'll find a way to see you later, okay?" he says in a low voice. "But now . . ."

He jerks his head again at Aunt Gwen. I rise reluctantly, sliding out of the booth, and take the box containing the pendant, which I slip into my jeans pocket.

"Don't you *dare* touch me again," I say to her between gritted teeth.

I stalk out of the coffee shop, pulling on my jacket. The waitress who brought our coffee and cake holds the door open for me, tutting, a sympathetic light in her eyes.

"Shame," I hear her say to another waitress as the door swings shut. "Such a nice young couple. Weren't doing any harm, were they?"

"You are to stay away from Jase Barnes from now on," Aunt Gwen commands as she unlocks the car. "Do you hear me?"

"Oh, I heard you," I say, dangerously angry. "What I'm not hearing is *why*."

"A Barnes and a Wakefield?" She gets in and starts the engine. "*Completely* socially unacceptable. What on earth do you think Mother would say?"

"I don't know," I reply as the car squeals away from the curb. Aunt Gwen is so worked up that she hasn't even looked in the mirrors before pulling out into the street. She's lucky this is a Sunday, with very little traffic on the roads. "Why don't we ask her?"

"*What?*" Aunt Gwen snaps.

"Why don't we ask Grandma? She'll be in her rooms. We could go and find her as soon as we get back to school."

It's a risk, I know. What if my grandmother agrees with Aunt Gwen? If she officially bans me from seeing Jase, he and I are really in trouble. It's she who pays his dad's salary and owns his dad's tied cottage. We couldn't ignore an edict from my grandmother.

But somehow, I don't think she's the kind of snob who'd make the same objection Aunt Gwen had just raised.

"We are *not* going to tell Mother a word about this," Aunt Gwen snips. "We are never going to mention the subject again. You have things easy at the moment, Scarlett. I let you live your own life and go your own way. I don't make you do much of anything around the house, or set curfews on you, or police your movements."

She drags at the wheel so hard on a turn that the car slews over too far and almost hits the curb.

"But if you disobey me," she continues, "everything will change. Mother, for whatever reason of her own, decided you were going to live with me, and that means I have control over you. Believe me, you don't want me to start exercising that control. I could make your life utterly and completely miserable if I wanted to."

Aunt Gwen has a scary reputation at Wakefield Hall. Taylor, who has her for geography, reports back regularly about Aunt Gwen's tirades; she's reduced more than a few

48

girls to tears in class. The thought of how bad she could make things for me, if she chooses to, chills my blood. I still want to stand up to her, tell her that she can't decide who I go out with, and that her objection to Jase is nothing more than pathetic, old-fashioned snobbery.

But what would that achieve, Scarlett? says a small voice inside my head. *You'd just start a war with her, and she's got all the power. You have to live with her till you finish school. That's a whole year and a half.*

Tell her what she wants to hear. Buy yourself some time to think this over.

"Okay, Aunt Gwen," I say sullenly.

"Okay *what?*"

"Okay, I'll stay away from Jase," I mumble.

"You'd better, young lady," she says malevolently. "If you know what's good for you."

Ugh. Aunt Gwen is not exactly the gracious winner our games teachers are always lecturing us to be.

We're passing through the high iron gates of Wakefield Hall now. Aunt Gwen veers immediately to the right, bringing the car to a halt in front of the gatehouse.

I jump out almost before the car stops.

"I'm going to the library," I say, slamming the car door shut behind me.

"Remember what I've told you," she calls after me. "There'll be no sneaking off to see that boy as soon as my back is turned. You live in my house, you obey my rules."

I bite my tongue so hard the tip swells up like a sponge.

The better part of valor is discretion, I tell myself. We're doing *Henry IV*, Parts One and Two, for English A-Level, and

49

our teacher has pointed this out as a really good quote to use in exam essays, because it isn't actually the same as people think it is: everyone says "Discretion is the better part of valor" instead. It means exactly the same, of course, but getting it right wins you brownie points in an exam.

Besides, it's a good quote. It means, more or less: Don't pick a fight you're probably not going to win.

Though of course, it's said by Falstaff, who's a big fat coward.

I hate running away from the fight with Aunt Gwen. It makes me feel like a big fat coward. I hate that she's dragged me away from my lovely afternoon out with Jase. I hate her so much I can taste it in my mouth like bitter medicine.

Striding into the Hall and up the main staircase, I head toward my grandmother's suite of rooms. I know I'll find her in her sitting room at this time of day, sipping Lapsang souchong and eating the wafer-thin almond tuile she allows herself at teatime. I pound down the corridor, my hand tight around the little wooden box in the pocket of my jeans. It's a physical reminder that Jase cares about me and wants us to be a couple as much as I do; it gives me strength and courage.

And I tell myself too that neither Aunt Gwen nor Mr. Barnes is exactly a model of perfect mental health or Zenlike balance. The two people objecting so strenuously to my and Jase's being together are, frankly, out of all the adults I know, the ones I least respect; they're angry, irrational, and they can't control themselves like adults are supposed to. Plus, they both seem incapable of having successful long-term relationships. Aunt Gwen, in all the years I remember, has never had a boyfriend (or a girlfriend), and Mr. Barnes, according to Jase, hasn't been with anyone since Jase's mother left him when Jase was barely six years old.

So how on earth are they remotely qualified to judge me and Jase as a couple, especially since we're doing absolutely nothing wrong?

I'm telling myself all this, bravely, as I stop in front of the door to my grandmother's—*Lady Wakefield's*—suite of rooms.

Sod discretion, I'm thinking angrily. *This just isn't fair. Aunt Gwen's gone too far. If I let her lay down the law to me like this, what will she stop me doing next? I have to stop this now, before this goes any further.*

And with this resolution, I raise my hand to knock on the door.

Only to have it swing open, away from me, and find myself staring straight at Mr. Barnes's red, swollen nose and flowering gin-blossom cheeks.

six

THE STRONGEST GIRL I KNOW

We read about gin blossoms in English class, though it could just as well have been history: gin was the cheap drink of the English urban lower classes in the late-nineteenth century. It was called Mother's Ruin, for obvious reasons, and even little kids would drink it to help them sleep, dull their hunger pangs (it was cheaper than food, believe it or not), or just escape the misery of their lives. If you kept on drinking gin, the capillaries on your face, which are the very small fine veins near the surface, would burst and give you away.

Certainly Mr. Barnes, with his nice, well-paid job-for-life and his tied cottage, has a lot less excuse than starving Dickensian orphans to be hitting the bottle. But his gin blossoms, a thick tracery of red veins on his cheeks, are very visible, as is his strawberry nose. Jase says his dad's preferred tipple is actually whisky, not gin, but clearly the effects are the same.

Once Jase told me that his dad was drop-dead gorgeous when he and Jase's mum got married. In fact, Jase said he looked like that actor from the old Star Wars films, Harrison

Ford. Tall, dark, and handsome. I believe him, because (a) Jase has never lied to me, and (b) Jase is so handsome himself (blush) that it only makes sense that his dad must have been really good-looking too.

It's sad that Mr. Barnes has drunk so much over the last eighteen years that you can barely imagine that once he was as handsome as a film star. I almost feel sorry for him. Or I would, if, when he got drunk, he weren't chasing us over the school grounds, waving his torch menacingly and calling me a whore. That kind of thing tends to cut down on the available sympathy I have for a person, I find.

Instinctively, I take a step back on finding myself so close to him. I'm sure that if Mr. Barnes is visiting my grandmother on a Sunday afternoon, he won't be stupid enough to be drunk while doing it. But drunk or sober, he still has a nasty temper, and he's a lot bigger than I am.

Sure enough, he's glaring at me from under his thick gray-flecked brows.

"I was just coming to see my grandmother," I say unnecessarily. Now it's pretty obvious that I'm very unnerved by him.

Mr. Barnes grunts something, and I take another step back, giving him plenty of room to move past me. He's dressed in the kind of Sunday best people wear in the country: an old tweed jacket, corduroy trousers, and a white shirt, certainly a step up from the mucky old clothes he and Jase wear when they're gardening. The smart (for him) clothes make him look more human, less like a monster who chases you in the dark. Bravely, I try my best to smile at him. Even more bravely, I say politely, as he grunts again and walks past me, down the corridor:

"Have a nice Sunday, Mr. Barnes."

God, what am I doing? I sound like an idiot. It's a bit too late to show him what good manners I have and what a nice girlfriend I'd make for his son. I hope I haven't sounded as if I'm mocking him.

It goes down like a lead balloon. Mr. Barnes swings around and raises his hand, pointing at me with a big gnarled finger. His hands are red and chapped from working outdoors in all kinds of weather.

"I've warned you already," he says hoarsely. "I don't want you near my son. You've been told enough times."

Then he turns and lumbers off down the corridor, his Sunday-best shoes squeaking on the polished boards.

My shoulders sag. It's not just because I messed up that encounter; it's because, for the life of me, I can't think of anything I could have said or done that would have been more successful. Mr. Barnes is a lost cause for me. As is Aunt Gwen.

This depressing thought makes me debate my impulse to visit my grandmother and talk to her about the situation with me and Jase. We've got two of the most important adults in our lives implacably opposed to our being together; it's too dangerous, as Taylor would put it, to run the risk of being 0 for 3. What if Lady Wakefield agrees with Aunt Gwen and Mr. Barnes? My grandmother is like God here at Wakefield Hall. No one dares to go against her will. She's a benevolent dictator, but cross her at your peril.

The heavy mahogany door to my grandmother's private quarters is on a slow release catch. It finally swings shut, the latch clicking into place with a small metallic sound. I let out the breath I didn't realize I was holding, in a long sigh.

I'm bottling it. The sight of Mr. Barnes has broken my resolve. I don't have the guts to march into my grandmother's private sanctum and demand she give Jase and me permission to see each other.

Gloomily, feeling beaten, I turn away and march off in the direction of the library, my hand closed tight around the little jewelry box in my pocket. And then an awful thought hits me: what was Mr. Barnes doing in my grandmother's quarters? I just assumed it was some estate-related business, her giving him his orders for the latest round of grounds maintenance.

But what if he went there to ask her to forbid me and Jase to date?

Oh God. I'm going to bury myself in the library till dinner time and do my very best not to think about anything but the research I'm doing for my latest history essay. Suddenly the short, brutal, torture-ridden reign of Bloody Mary Tudor looks a positively cheerful prospect by comparison with my own existence. . . .

* * *

Rats. I forgot it was red bean chili and rice for dinner tonight. That means only one thing. I need to get my piece in first, before Taylor has a chance to comment.

"I know!" I say, sliding in to sit next to her on the long bench as the dinner ladies thunk down big serving dishes of steaming chili and boiled white rice at either end of the Lower Sixth Form table. "This is *totally* not chili in any recognizable shape or form. If a Texan turned up here for dinner

55

by some freak accident, they would have a heart attack at us dumb Brits having the *audacity* to call this horrible, bland food chili. Because it bears absolutely *no* resemblance to proper American red bean chili, which is spicy and tasty and ooh, talking of which, did you bring your—"

Taylor reaches into her pocket and pulls out her prized possessions: three bottles of Tabasco sauce, which she places on the table in front of her.

"Not that you deserve any," she says, grinning, "but I'll share these with you just 'cause I feel nothing but pity for you dumb Brits and your horrible bland food."

"Thank you." I grab my favorite, the habanero Tabasco, and apply it liberally to the sludgy reddish chili. "It's just, you say the same thing every time we have chili, and I thought I'd get in first for a change."

"They put *ketchup* in it!" Taylor says, agonized. "They cook chili with *ketchup* in this freaky godforsaken country! I mean, I'm from *Pennsylvania*, which is, like, farther from Texas than this tiny little island is from, I dunno, *Australia*, and even *I* know you don't put ketchup in chili."

"It does taste a lot better with the Tabasco," I admit.

"Everything tastes better with Tabasco," Taylor says sweepingly, drenching her own heaped plate with a carefully calculated mixture of the habanero and chipotle Tabascos. Then she adds a few swirls of the green one on top for decorative effect.

"Oh, look at Scarlett and Taylor. Aren't they *sweet?*" Plum's voice echoes from the center of the table. Her super-posh accent, clipped and cutting, not only carries effortlessly but slices through the rest of the chatter too, interrupting everyone else's conversations. "What a lovely couple they make! What are they sharing—hot sauce?"

I can't help but admire the amount of twist Plum manages to put on the words *hot sauce*. She's like a tennis ace, slicing a ball so it spins in the air, going places her opponent can't anticipate. Girls down the table start sniggering automatically.

"Does Jase Barnes know you're sharing Taylor's *hot sauce?*" Plum continues, smiling triumphantly. "Isn't he jealous? I mean, Taylor's the closest thing we've got to a boy at school— apart from Sharon Persaud, I suppose."

Sharon Persaud, surrounded by the other members of the hockey and lacrosse squads, glowers at Plum. I wouldn't like to get Sharon angry; she's built like a brick shithouse, to use a rugby term, and has already taken out several girls' front teeth with her legendary lavender hockey stick. But Plum thinks she's above us all here at Wakefield Hall, an exotic orchid in a field of common daisies and dandelions. She doesn't care who she pisses off.

"No offense, Sharon," Plum trills, flashing a smile at her. "It's just that your legs are so *marvelously* robust. But you're not *butch*, like Taylor over there. I mean, just look at her."

I feel Taylor's whole body stiffen.

"If I were Jase, I'd be wondering what you two get up to when you're alone," Plum carries on. "I mean, you and Taylor *do* spend a lot of time together getting hot and sweaty, don't you, Scarlett?"

More nervous giggles are triggered by this sally. I sigh. I really just wanted a quiet dinner; I've got enough going on in my life without dealing with Plum's latest bitch offensive.

But keeping my head down won't cut it with her. I tried that when we were at St. Tabby's together, and it wasn't exactly a successful strategy; it just encouraged her to go even further.

"Wow, Plum, you're obsessed with Taylor, aren't you?" I retort. "Honestly, it sounds like *you're* the one who'd like to share some hot sauce with her!" I turn to Taylor. "Taylor, what do you say? Why don't you take Plum for a run sometime? She could do with being a bit less spindly, and it sounds like she'd *love* to get sweaty with you."

This goes down very well with the sporty crowd, who don't like Plum's attack on Sharon, their de facto leader. They laugh obligingly, shifting to see Plum's reaction.

By now, pretty much the entire Lower Sixth table has abandoned any pretense of conversation and is listening avidly. What a bore. The system in the dining hall—each year of girls seated at one very long wooden table, benches on each side, like something out of an Oxbridge college—usually works very well, because no one is isolated. Everyone from that year has to sit together, but you can save spaces for friends, or squash up if you need to. The arty people sit together, the sporty ones ditto; it's generally friendly, with girls making room for other people's friends if they want to swap places.

Or it was, until Plum arrived, took one look at the setup, and decided that she was going to rule the Lower Sixth dining table, as she did everything else in her life. Since she came to Wakefield Hall, Taylor and I have picked seats as close to the end of the table as possible, trying to stay out of her way. And it's worked fairly well so far—or it did last term, when Plum was still establishing her position.

But she came back from the Christmas holidays loaded for bear. It's as if she feels that she's achieved full princess status now; she's taken her throne and she's going to make us bow down to her, whether we like it or not.

Seated on either side of her are Lizzie and Susan. Lizzie's cleaving to Plum I understand, as Lizzie's always been a big suck-up, and very weak-willed; she'll automatically run around after the strongest personality she can find. While Susan—well, that's very clever of Plum. Susan is such a natural beauty that she could be a dangerous rival to Plum. I'm sure a lot of the younger girls have huge crushes on her. By bringing her into her circle, letting her sit beside her, Plum is taking the power of Susan's beauty and incorporating it into her own.

"Want to share, Plum? Want some of Taylor's hot sauce?" I pick up one of the Tabasco bottles and wave it in Plum's direction, waggling my eyebrows suggestively at her.

Sharon Persaud grins at me encouragingly. I'm on a roll.

And then I feel a sharp, stiff nudge in my ribs. Wow, Taylor really doesn't know her own strength. I have to brace myself with my quads to stop myself being knocked sideways. I look over at Taylor to see what the hell she's doing. Her head is ducked, but she glares up at me briefly through her shaggy fringe, a tiny shake of her head indicating very clearly that she doesn't want me to take this any further.

I'm baffled. Taylor is usually tough as nails. This defeated stance of hers is completely unprecedented. I lower the Tabasco bottle to the table, my next planned salvo dying on my lips, and Plum, who's used to this kind of verbal fencing and very fast to sense weakness, jumps right in.

"Ooh, did Taylor give you that necklace?" she asks nastily. "I haven't seen it before. Was it a love token? How sweet! Shame she couldn't afford anything better."

I haven't even had a chance to show Taylor Jase's necklace yet; I just put it on before dinner. It looks lovely, delicate in design, with the blue stone exactly matching my eyes, and I keep touching it in sheer pleasure. That might have been what called Plum's attention to it. She's as sharp as a whip.

"It's an aquamarine," I snap, my hand rising up to touch my necklace protectively, and that's it, that's the moment I let down my guard and she disarms me and pins me against the wall.

"Oh, *please*. Is that what your girlfriend told you? They barely *ever* cut aquamarines that shape. It's cubic zirconia, I can tell from here," Plum says gleefully, slicing her rapier in and twisting it for good measure. "Though really, semiprecious stones, cubic zirconia, who cares? Cheap cheap cheap."

Lizzie Livermore, the richest girl at the table, giggles obediently, fiddling with one of her platinum-set solitaire earrings.

"I mean, these are just glass." Plum fiddles with the silvered-bead bracelets at her wrists. "Murano glass, of course, hand-blown. I got them in Venice over the holidays. But they're not pretending to be something else. They're just *glass*. I mean, I'm not wearing *cubic zirconia* and pretending it's *aquamarine!*"

Oh, she's horrible. I'm trembling with anger. But Plum's voice went up even further as she delivered the killing blow, and it's attracted attention she won't enjoy. Miss Newman, our form teacher, walks across the dining hall, hands clasped

60

behind her back, from the Upper Third table, where she's probably been making a few little girls cry, just because she can.

She doesn't even need to open her mouth to make small girls cry, because Miss Newman is so incredibly hairy that her appearance is intimidating enough in itself. She only has one eyebrow, which is as bushy as a shrubbery, more than a shadow of a matching mustache, and there are thick black wires sprouting from the moles on her chin. The only reason for her not plucking them has to be the terror they provoke in anyone who looks at her.

"Plum Saybourne, will you *please* lower your voice?" booms Miss Newman. "You are a young lady, not a hooligan. And"—Miss Newman leans in for a closer look at Plum— "you're *plastered* in makeup, my girl. That is *absolutely* against Wakefield Hall dress regulations. You look like a . . . night-club hostess!"

Sometimes it really is funny how sheltered Wakefield Hall and its teachers are. I mean, that's obviously Miss Newman's euphemism for "cheap prostitute," and it's so old-fashioned that a lot of the girls start snickering.

Miss Newman, however, has been one of the head jailers at Wakefield Hall Maximum Security Prison for Young Ladies for countless decades; she's much too experienced a disciplinarian to even acknowledge the laughing.

"Go immediately to your room and wipe all that makeup off your face," she orders Plum. "Then come back here for inspection. I know Sixth Formers are allowed some latitude in their dress, but it is going much too far to *daub* yourself with makeup like a French *bar girl from the docks*."

"Ooh la la!" I quip, just loud enough for the girls sitting opposite me to hear, and the snickers rise in volume.

Plum knows I've made a joke at her expense. I can tell from the venomous look she shoots me.

Still, thank God for Miss Newman. I think she's made us even. Plum scored with cubic zirconia, but her being called a French bar girl from the docks will run and run, if I have anything to do with it.

Under Miss Newman's beady gaze, Plum wriggles off the bench and strides, as fast as she can in her tight jeans, around the table in the direction of the door. As she passes me and Taylor, she leans over and whispers vindictively:

"Your grandma didn't say anything about not telling *Jase Barnes* about Dan, Scarlett. I wonder how much he'd like you if he knews you killed someone."

I gasp, but by the time I've recovered from the shock, Plum is already crossing the room, her slender, trendily dressed figure drawing admiring glances from most of the younger girls, who stare after her, eyes wide and full of heroine-worship. Knowing the attention is on her, Plum tosses back her hair theatrically as she exits the dining hall.

I look at Taylor, but her head is still ducked over her plate of chili.

"Don't take Plum on, Scarlett," she says quietly. "Or she'll make you sorry."

I want to ask Taylor why she's acting like a frightened mouse all of a sudden, but I'm too scared. If Plum can intimidate Taylor, the strongest girl I know, what's going to become of the rest of us?

seven

SNEAKING OUT

I look like a cat burglar. Which is exactly the idea. I'm dressed in black from head to toe; black polo-neck sweater, black jeans (with a bit of stretch in them so I can climb anything I need to), and black trainers. I stare at myself in my bedroom mirror. Because my hair is almost black too, my face and hands are the only white things about me, floating eerily in the darkened room.

It's a quarter past ten, and Aunt Gwen thinks I'm having an early night. But I'm not. I'm sneaking out to see Jase.

I want to see him so badly my whole body's burning up.

Maybe if I'd been able to talk to Taylor after dinner, I could have let off some steam. I wanted so much to hang out with her, pour out all my frustration, tell her about the awful scene Aunt Gwen made today in the coffee shop, her threats, and then, to cap it off, bumping into Mr. Barnes outside my grandmother's suite. But she's gone all weird on me. Instead of drinking hot chocolate in her room after dinner like usual (tragically, this is what counts as debauchery here at Wakefield Hall. Or it did, before Plum came along. Right now they're probably all drinking cocktails, popping prescription pills, and taking photos of each other starkers), Taylor said she had a ton of geography homework to do and slunk off in the direction of the dormitory block. I'm not ashamed to say that I pleaded with her. I really needed her company, and I felt very alone. But nothing I said had any effect.

I'm pretty sure that it's Plum who's wound her up like this; what's baffling is *why*. Taylor is supertough and supercool. Very little bothers her, and if it does she tends to respond with maximum force. She says she wants to be a PI (which is a private investigator, in America), but secretly, the more I get to know her, the more I think she's better suited to a job that involves a lot of jumping out of planes, breaking down doors, and kicking people's bums. Or asses, as she would say.

So it's even more of a mystery that my best and only friend, who's so reluctant to back down from anything that she'd challenge Wonder Woman to an arm-wrestling match, is knuckling under to Plum.

I know how Plum operates by now. She likes to find your weakness and torment you with it. The only possible theory I can formulate is that Plum has some dirt on Taylor, and she's let Taylor know about it, which is why Taylor won't take Plum on.

But what could it possibly be? Taylor, as far as I know, is squeaky clean.

I shake my head, hard. It's a mystery, but not one I have time to solve at the moment. I file it away in the back of my brain for later. Maybe a solution will pop into my head when I'm least expecting it: that happens sometimes.

For now, I've got to focus on the task ahead. Being a cat burglar. Sort of. Jase is going to meet me at the barn at ten-thirty, and I have to get out of here without Aunt Gwen having the slightest idea I'm sneaking out.

I opened the window hours ago, which was clever of me, because even though it's been cold in here, there won't be any telltale squeaking now to announce that I'm about to climb out onto the sill. I sit there, legs hanging, and swiftly run over my options. There's a big oak tree ten feet away from the house, and one of its branches reaches close to the window. I used to climb along it when I was small, but that was back in the days when I was a little skinny, spindly monkey, before I got my period and the boobs and hips that came along with it. I seriously don't think that branch will bear my weight now.

Aunt Gwen is watching telly in the living room below. The last thing I want is for her viewing of *Antiques Roadshow* to be interrupted by a huge crash from outside as a branch snaps under me and I hit the ground, snapping some bones in the process. And what with me dressed like a cat burglar, I can hardly claim that I was sleepwalking. Or sleepclimbing.

Once, I threw myself out of this window, caught and swung off a farther branch, and hit the ground running. I was chasing Taylor, believe it or not. But that was in daylight, when I could see clearly where I was aiming, and I took a run at it and probably made more noise than a stampeding herd of elephants. Even if noise weren't a factor, I don't trust myself to carry off that jump in the dark safely. I did gymnastics for years, and at the level at which I was competing, it's all about calculated risk. Can I do that backflip on a beam and land on my feet, not my head? I think I can, and so does my coach. So off I go, and try not to break my neck.

Looking at that far branch, a dim shadow in the dark night, I don't think I can. So I won't be risking it. Though there's soft yielding grass below, it's too high to jump safely. So that leaves only one option.

The drainpipe.

A clock is ticking in my mind. Jase is waiting for me, and I have to get going. I scooch along the windowsill to the right, till I feel the drainpipe with my feet. Reaching out gingerly, I pull at it, gently at first and then harder, as hard as I can without falling off the windowsill: I have to be sure it'll hold my weight.

It groans, metal under strain, but it barely budges from the wall. I'm banking on the fact that my grandmother is very strict about maintenance on Wakefield Hall and all its surrounding cottages and barns and outbuildings. Aunt Gwen is very precise too. I don't think either of them will have let the drainpipe on the gatekeeper's cottage get rusty enough to come away from the wall.

Time to put my money where my mouth is.

I'm still holding the drainpipe, and now I wrap my hands around it, feeling for the bolt that anchors it to the wall, digging my fingers in to stabilize my grip as I wriggle my bottom right off the edge of the windowsill. I shoot my knees out toward the pipe, clamping onto it as soon as they close over it, so tightly my bones hurt straightaway with the pressure.

A split second later, my entire body is supported only by my death grip on the drainpipe, fingers and knees straining.

Aaaaaah, a voice in my head is saying very loudly. *Aaaaaah. I don't like this one little bit.*

Shut up, I say back. *It's too late now. And you're distracting me.*

My wrists are locked strongly around the pipe, strongly enough so that I can release my knees a fraction and slide them down a foot or so, as far as I can safely go. I clamp them again once they're in place and then, very cautiously, take one hand off the pipe—my left, the weaker one—and bring it down, again, as far as I can go, feeling for another bolt, a stud, anything that will give me enough purchase to hold on to it.

Nothing. The pipe is completely smooth and slippery. My fingers slide right down it. Panicking a little, I reach out farther, to the wall, and mercifully, scrabbling along the bricks, I find I can just get the tips of my fingers between two of them.

It's lucky I'm not one of those girls who worry about the state of their fingernails.

I squash myself flat against the pipe, bracing myself with the fingers of my left hand crammed between the bricks, as, gingerly, I unwrap my right hand from the bolt above me. I don't have enough purchase to go along the wall to find another gap in the bricks, so in desperation I shove my whole hand around the pipe and manage to make a sort of hook with my elbow, as if I'm giving the drainpipe a really clumsy hug. But it's enough to keep me upright, and as I unwedge my aching left hand from between the bricks, I manage, using my thigh muscles, to slide down the pipe inch by inch, the crook of my right arm bracing me around the pipe and taking some of the strain off my knees. I try to dig my feet into the pipe, but the rubber on my shoes catches on the metal and slows my progress, which is the last thing I want.

Ow. Ow ow ow. My knees are being rubbed painfully raw by my jeans. I chance a quick look over my shoulder; it's too dark out for me to see the ground, but I'm below the tree branches now, and that should just about mean I'm close enough . . .

Thrusting back against the wall with my left hand, I unwind the right one and push off clumsily, launching myself back as far as I can. I'm aiming for the grass, not the flower beds, and though it's by no means a clean landing—I turn a foot and have to roll over it to avoid twisting my ankle— when I catch my breath and look around me, I'm on the grass, well clear of the lavender beds below my window, and I'm almost sure the pipe didn't make any telltale creaking sounds as I shoved away from it.

The lights are on in Aunt Gwen's living room, the curtains drawn, the blue flicker of the TV showing faintly through the crack between them. I listen closely for half a minute, but all I hear is a commercial for some yogurt that will keep you regular and banish bloating. Aunt Gwen doesn't turn the sound down or get up and look out of the window.

I've made it. I feel a small hot explosion of relief, like a firecracker going off in my head.

This is only the start, though, I tell myself, rising to my feet. *Don't get cocky. You still have to get back and forth from the barn without crazy Mr. Barnes catching you.*

And then you have to climb back in again.

I take a long loop through the grounds, around the back of the main hall, past the lake enclosure, over the hockey fields, across Lime Walk, around the netball courts, and over the fence that marks the boundary beyond which Wakefield Hall girls are not allowed to go.

Having grown up and played here for years and years all by myself in the school holidays, I know the grounds so well I could pretty much run through them blindfolded. I never thought this familiarity would come in so useful. Plus, my regular runs with Taylor, who sets a punishing pace, have ensured that I'm fitter than I've ever been.

All of which I'm hugely grateful for. Because now that I'm so close to seeing Jase, I feel that my heart's about to explode out of my chest with excitement and anticipation.

Me and Jase, together, in the dark, where no one can interrupt us or break in on us or pull us away from each other.

I literally cannot wait.

I make it to the barn in under ten minutes, my breath not even coming that fast. As I skid to a halt, turning my trainers on the roughly packed dirt surrounding the barn, I feel as if I'm having an out-of-body experience, as if I'm floating out of my own skin. I want to be with Jase right now, this instant, in his arms, hugging him, breathing in his scent, feeling the solid, muscular heft of his chest rise and fall, his arms as tight around me as mine are around him . . .

"Jase?" I whisper. "Jase?"

No answer. I'm sure that in his text he said to meet outside the barn, and I pad up to the wall, touching it, feeling for the loose planks, making sure I'm in the right place.

Sure enough, one of the planks comes away in my hands

as soon as I try to move it. I look inside the pitch-black interior and whisper:

"Jase?" My voice is absorbed instantly into the darkness. Not a single echo. It's soaked up as if I'd never breathed a word.

I'm about five minutes late, but that doesn't mean anything. Jase certainly won't have come and gone already.

Maybe his dad's kicking up a fuss, and Jase needs to wait till he's gone to bed, or passed out. Maybe something else has come up that's delayed him. I lean against the wall of the barn, and wait.

That's the really annoying thing. You say you can't bear to wait, you feel like you'll burst if you have to hold out a moment longer to see your boyfriend. But then he isn't there, and you have to do what you thought you could never manage: you have to wait for him, even though it's agony and you want to scratch your arms up with whatever nails you have left just to get a bit of the frustration out.

I didn't bring my phone. I didn't think I'd need it: all I needed to know was that I had a rendezvous with Jase at ten-thirty. Now, of course, I'm kicking myself black and blue for not having my phone on me.

Did he get here early? I think, my brain racing. *Did he get here so early that he thought he'd wait for me inside, go up to the loft, and maybe fall asleep on the blankets?*

I know it's incredibly unlikely, especially as the planks are leaning in place against the hole in the barn wall, but the waiting is driving me mad. I slide the plank farther aside and crawl in through the hole, feeling in my pocket for the tiny torch attached to my key ring, pulling it out, and clicking it on. It throws out a beam only a few inches wide, barely enough to see my hand in front of my face, and if I hadn't been to the barn before, if I didn't know my way around, it wouldn't be any use at all.

As it is, it gets me across the barn without crashing into the tractor, and up the ladder. I know Jase isn't up in the loft, curled up in a warm nest of hay, wrapped in blankets, fast asleep, waiting for me to curl up next to him so he can throw an arm over me while we cuddle together. I know it's a total fantasy.

And of course it is. He's not there. There's no one in this barn but me.

Eventually, I emerge. The night air is cold after the shelter of the barn, and still Jase is nowhere to be seen. I squat down miserably to wait some more, my ears pricked to hear any movement, any footfalls that could possibly, conceivably, be Jase running across the grass to keep our appointment.

It's past eleven by my watch when I stop being upset that he's not here and start to be scared for him.

What if he's having a fight with his dad? I think, rising to my feet. *What if something really bad's happening at their cottage?*

I know it's not a good idea. I should go back to Aunt Gwen's instead, climb up to my room, check my phone and see if Jase has been trying to get in touch. But as soon as the image pops into my head of Jase and his dad, fighting, as I saw them once before by the lake when Jase was trying to protect me, I can't leave it alone.

I can hear the yelling from the Barnes cottage as I approach, and my feelings are incredibly mixed. I'd recognize Jase's voice anywhere, so I know that's him, shouting at his dad, and although I hate that they're fighting, I'm also hugely, stupidly relieved that it was this that kept Jase from coming out to meet me. Not that he doesn't care about me, or that he met someone else.

I know it's probably ridiculous to have these insecurities, and that they're much more to do with me than they are with Jase. I don't bang on about them to him. But every so often I look at a girl like Susan, or Plum, if I'm honest, and I do think: *God, there are so many girls out there prettier than me. And Jase is so gorgeous. What if he wakes up one day and realizes that he could have any girl he wants?*

The curtains at the downstairs windows are all drawn. I can't see anything.

"For the last time, you're not going anywhere, boy!" Mr. Barnes's unmistakable bellow rattles the windowpanes.

"Dad, I just want to get some fresh air—"

"You're a liar!"

This is bad. I can't bear the frustration of not being able to see inside. Desperately, I look around for an elevated area, because the curtains are those old-fashioned ones, like they have in the coffee shop, that only cover the lower part of the window; the upper panes are clear, light pouring through them.

There's a cherry tree behind me. Not ideal, because it has whippy, thin branches, which bend and buckle under me and aren't wide enough to sit on in any comfort. But I swarm up it in record time, and wedge myself into a really awkward, narrow V by the trunk, my bottom braced between two branches, each only a few inches wide. They cut into me, but I wrap my arms around a higher branch, pulling myself up to take a little strain off the ones I'm sitting on, and twist so I get a good view down into the cottage.

The Barnes cottage is as old-fashioned as its gingham curtains. It still has the original layout, with a central staircase and a kitchen on one side, probably with the bathroom beyond it to keep all the plumbing together, and a living room on the other. I can see the living room, the foot of the stairs, and a good chunk of the kitchen. And I can see Jase, standing by the door, his motorbike jacket on, yelling:

"I can go out for a walk if I want to! I'll be up for college in the morning!"

"Don't give me that!" shouts his father. I spot Mr. Barnes, his bulky body propped up in a recliner, his face red and swollen, his fist raised. "You're going out to moon round after that Wakefield girl! I know you, Jase Barnes!"

"So what!" Jase sounds really angry. "Even if I am, what's it got to do with you?"

He swings around, reaching for the door. This provokes Mr. Barnes, who levers himself up to his feet, his face distended with rage, and yells:

"Don't you turn your back on me when I'm talking to you!"

Jase cranes back, and I see anger in his face, his eyes blazing gold with fury. It's the first time I've ever seen him like this, and it shocks me, even scares me a little, because I can tell he's itching for a fight.

"Or what, Dad?" Jase says, taking a step toward his father.

"D'you want me to take a belt to you, like I did when you were little? Do you?" his father shouts, swaying on his feet. "You're not too old to feel the back of my hand!"

"Oh yes I am! Want me to prove it to you?" Jase yells back.

My breath catches as I see that Jase's hands are clenched into fists.

And at that moment, someone pushes past Jase and interposes her small body between him and his father.

It's Jase's grandmother. I've rarely been so grateful to see anyone in my life.

"That's *enough!*" she pipes in a high, eldritch voice. "I won't have this shouting, you hear me? I'm sick of it! Kevin, the boy's grown now. He's too old for this kind of nonsense, can't you see that?"

"*Nonsense?*" Jase says bitterly.

"And you, keep a civil tongue in your head," his grandmother says, turning on him.

White hair piled messily on top of her head, little wire-framed glasses shoved high up her nose, her dowager's hump bowing her spine, she looks tiny and frail between the bulk of Jase's father and Jase himself, with his height and his square shoulders. She's wearing a floral winceyette dressing gown, a white nightie showing at the neck, and she's resting heavily on her stick, both hands pressed down on it; clearly she'd topple over if it were taken away from her.

But she's managing to keep the peace between these two warring men, so she's obviously not as fragile as she looks.

"No more fighting!" she shrills at them.

"He's going against me!" her son yells back. "I've *told* him to stay away from that little Wakefield tart, but he was out with her just last night. I caught them outside, the dirty little—"

"I've told you not to call her that," Jase says dangerously, taking another step toward his father.

Part of me, furious that Mr. Barnes is being so rude about me, is elated that Jase is so quick to defend my honor. But the older, sensible, saner part of me is incredibly grateful that Jase's grandmother is blocking his way to his dad. Because from the look in Jase's eyes, it'd be murder if he reached him.

"Kevin, *stop* it. You'll just set him off!" she screams.

"Oh, will I now?" Over his mother's head, Mr. Barnes scowls at Jase. "She's a little tart, I tell you. Just like her mum was. Knew it as soon as I laid eyes on her. She was no better than she should be and her daughter's just the same. She might look like a Wakefield, but she acts like the cheap little tart who thought she had it all because she'd got herself Sir Patrick Wakefield!" He snorts.

I'm shocked beyond speech. My fingers are clamped onto the branch so tightly that I'm losing sensation, numb with cold, but my blood is pounding and the core of my body is burning up with anger.

How dare he talk about my mother and me like that? How *dare* he? I want to burst in there right now and tear his head off with my bare hands.

But a fight is just what Mr. Barnes wants. I can see it in the bullish thrust of his head, the nasty glint in his piggish little eyes. His hands are clenched into fists too, and now he raises one, making a beckoning gesture to Jase.

"Got you angry now, haven't I?" he taunts. "Well, come on then, boy! Let's see what you're made of."

"I'm going to call the police," his mother threatens. "Kevin, I'm going to call the police if you don't stop this *right now*! Jase, go upstairs and stay there. And Kevin, *sit down*! You've gone too far!"

But Jase doesn't go upstairs. He ducks his head, shaking it from side to side, rolling out his shoulders. I can tell he's getting control of himself, coming back from the brink. And then he turns on his heel, strides across to the door, and wrenches it open.

I try to scramble down from the tree to intercept him, tell him I'm here. But the narrow branches, hard to see in the dark, make my maneuvers fatally slow, and I can't call to him, as I've already seen how voices carry out here. The last thing I want is his dad storming out again and catching us together.

So my ankle gets stuck and I have to drag it free, and by the time I've hopped clumsily to the ground, the roar of Jase's motorbike is burning through the night, his taillight flaring red as he takes off at full blast.

I stand there, staring after him, a huge pain spreading across my chest. *He didn't come to find me. He had a huge fight with his dad, about me, and he didn't come to find me for comfort afterward.*

That's really hard to bear.

Jase slammed the door of the cottage so hard when he walked out that it bounced against the jamb and right back open again. Through the gap, I see his grandmother hobble across the living room to a shelving unit on the staircase wall.

"There!" she says, grabbing a bottle of cheap blended whisky from the unit and shoving it at her son. "Drink that till you pass out. The only way your mouth shut's when it's wrapped round a bottle."

76

She throws a look of complete disdain at her son as he slumps sullenly back into his armchair, grabbing the bottle of whisky. He turns the TV on with the remote control. The reflected light flickers on his face, blue and red and green flashes livid on his sagging jowls. There's a plastic cup next to him, and he's tipping some whisky into it, bringing the cup to his mouth. His mother turns to look toward the open door, the lenses of her glasses gleaming as she stares out into the night.

I catch my breath, because it looks as if she's gazing straight at me. And then she stumps toward the door.

I think she's going to close it, but she doesn't. Instead, she walks outside, onto the wooden step, and pulls the door shut behind her, dragging her dressing gown tighter around her shoulders against the night air.

"Scarlett Wakefield! I know you're there," she hisses. "Get over here right now, young woman! I've got a few words to say to you."

eight

SOMETHING'S VERY WRONG HERE

I stand in front of the cottage, frozen in shock, unable to believe she's actually spotted me under the tree. And then she raises one hand and points at me, her eyes narrowed behind the lenses of her glasses, then crooks her finger. It's pretty scary, almost as if she's cursing me or something. I'm panicked that she's going to start yelling for her son, and he'll come pounding out the front door with a pitchfork aimed at my head. But also, I really want to hear what she has to say. Maybe she can shed some light on this mad situation.

So I walk forward, slowly, on the balls of my feet, poised for flight if I need to take off suddenly. It's hard to read her expression. Still, her posture—both hands propped on her cane now, shoulders hunched forward—isn't exactly welcoming. I swallow hard and can't help shifting nervously from one foot to the other.

"I was just looking for Jase," I begin feebly. "I'm sorry, I know it's late, but I was worried about him."

"As you should be," she retorts instantly. "You've brought a world of trouble down on his shoulders."

I remember when I saw this woman earlier today at the cottage window, I thought she was the picture of what you imagine a sweet old grandmother to be. But close up, Jase's grandmother is definitely not sweet. She's positively glaring at me, her mouth dragged down at the corner. Her expression is downright malevolent, in fact.

I gather up my courage and ask the crucial question. I've got nothing to lose here and a great deal to gain.

"Why is Jase's dad so against me and Jase being together?" I ask her.

She bridles, her hands tightening on the wooden top of her cane.

"*Wakefields,*" she spits, as if my very surname were an insult in itself. "Think you can have everything, don't you? Just reach out a hand and take a Barnes man if you want one, never mind what everyone else has to say about it! You're all the same—think the entire world revolves around you."

"No, I don't," I protest defensively.

"Look at you," she continues, pointing at me again. "Just the same airs and graces as your dad, not to mention that old witch up at the Hall."

I gape, unable to believe she's talking about my grandmother like this.

"Wakefield's been nothing but trouble for this family," she says resentfully. "I wanted to leave years ago, when his dad died. I'd worked my fingers to the bone for the Wakefields, and so did my mother before me. I'd had enough of it. But Kevin wouldn't hear of going. 'Don't you worry, Mum, I've got big plans for us here at the Hall,' he'd say. 'You'll be amazed, you will.'" She laughs bitterly. "The only thing that amazes me about Kevin is how much bloody booze he can put away."

She looks straight at me.

"And now it's all happening again, isn't it? Jase, running after a Wakefield girl. Well, not if I can help it."

All happening again? I open my mouth to ask what she means, but she's riding roughshod over me.

"Leave Jase alone and find yourself one of your own kind. A rich white boy," his grandmother snaps.

I gawp at her.

"Are you serious? No one thinks like that anymore."

"Your grandmother does, I'm willing to bet," she retorts. "She won't want any black babies inheriting the Hall. Have you seen Jason's mum? She's dark. Black as the ace of spades. You think Lady Wakefield wants that in the family? *I* certainly didn't."

God, she really is an awful old woman. The racism leaves me speechless with shock and revulsion.

"You won't be warned again," she says. "Stay away from Jason. If you don't it'll be the worst mistake of your life—just like when Kevin got mixed up with the likes of your wretched family!"

She pulls the door open, hobbles through it, and slams it in my face.

I stand there, staring at the door, unable to process what just happened.

My wretched family, I think. *She said it's all happening again. Maybe Jase's dad went after a Wakefield girl, just like his son.*

I discount Aunt Gwen immediately. If Jase is right in

saying that Mr. Barnes looked like a hot film actor when he was younger—well, I've seen all the family photo albums, and believe me, no way would a tall, dark, and handsome Mr. Barnes ever have been attracted to Aunt Gwen.

Which leaves my mother. Who, technically, was a Wakefield only by marriage. But she was gorgeous. Everyone says so. I can see it in the photos, too. Some people can be stunning but not photogenic, but my mother was both. She had a smile that could light up a room. I love to look at pictures of her.

And now I think about it, she was a distant relative of my dad's. A third cousin or something. They met at a huge family reunion. Her surname wasn't Wakefield, but they were definitely related in some way, far back down the family tree. . . .

A shiver runs down my spine like a spray of ice-cold water.

If I keep going down this path, there's a very bad dark place just ahead of me. I can tell.

Every bone in my body is telling me to leave this one alone. So I do. I take a deep breath and turn away from the cottage, breaking into a run, heading back to Aunt Gwen's and my bedroom, where my phone is sitting on my desk, hopefully loaded with messages from Jase.

• • •

"And is he okay?" Taylor asks as I get to this point in the story. We're jogging, halfway through our circuit of the grounds, the air blissfully cool on our faces, the sky gray and overcast.

"Yes, he finally texted me," I puff, "but not for ages. I stayed up, waiting."

Taylor clicks her tongue against her teeth.

"That sucks," she says frankly. "When you'd been waiting for him out by the barn and everything."

"I know. But it was really bad, Taylor. I haven't even told you everything his father said. He was awful about my mum, and he called me a tart."

"You're *kidding*!" Taylor actually stops dead in her tracks during a run, something I have never, ever seen her do before. She wipes her forehead with the sleeve of her Cornell sweatshirt, staring at me, her breath coming fast but evenly. "He talked about your *mom*? What does she have to do with this?"

"I've got no idea," I say, having halted too.

"What does Jase have to say about it?"

I sigh. "I haven't had the chance to talk to him. He just sent me this short text last night saying he needed to take off on his bike 'cause his dad was on his back, and I haven't heard from him at all today."

"Ugh, that's tough." Taylor looks at me sympathetically. "You know, he's probably really messed up, with his dad acting like this."

"Not just his dad," I say gloomily. "I talked to his grandmother afterward and she not only told me to stay away, she said all these racist things as well."

"*What?*"

"That my grandmother wouldn't want any black grandchildren," I mutter awkwardly.

"That is *disgusting*!" Taylor exclaims, her eyes widening. She shakes back her fringe from her forehead, where it's sticking with sweat. "No wonder Jase is acting weird with you. I mean, if that were my family and my girlfriend was seeing them do and say all this stuff, I'd *die* of embarrassment."

Sweat is cooling in the small of my back, cold and clammy under my T-shirt and running hoodie. Cold and clammy is exactly how I feel when I say, in a very small voice:

"I'm just scared he'll think it isn't worth it. All this aggro. What if he breaks up with me because of it?"

Taylor grimaces, but she doesn't say anything reassuring, because, honestly, there isn't anything she can say to make me feel better. Taylor's a realist, not a romantic: she knows that what I'm saying is not at all unlikely. This situation with Jase's family is beyond messed up, and it might be beyond my and Jase's abilities to cope with it.

Awkwardly, she reaches out and pats me on the shoulder. I try to sketch a smile. This is the first chance we've had to talk all day, our lunchtime run, and I've been wanting to ask her if anything is going on with her and Plum. I've been trying all morning to frame the question in a tactful way, but nothing's popped into my head yet that sounds remotely good enough.

Just as I'm racking my brain for the right words, my attention's caught by something I see over Taylor's arm.

We've come to a halt by the high iron fence that runs around the lake, put up as a safety precaution when my grandmother turned Wakefield Hall into a school. There's a big wrought-iron gate set into it, but it's always kept locked. Jase and I sneaked in once, last term, but that's because he had a key, and he locked it behind us when we were inside: that's the rule when any gardening or maintenance work is

83

being done, to make sure none of the girls can wander inside and get locked in.

In all the time I've spent roaming the Wakefield Hall grounds, I've never seen that gate hanging open before. Not even out of term time, when no one but me is around.

There's something funny going on here.

I lean past Taylor and push on the gate. It creaks open under my hand.

Perhaps the single best thing about having Taylor as a friend is that she can a hundred percent be relied on to never say: *We shouldn't, It's not allowed,* or *We'll get into trouble.*

Of course, the downside about Taylor is that she's infinitely more likely to say: *Just let go and drop, you'll be fine!* or *I'll distract the doorman while you sneak in past him and climb into the service elevator!* Or:

"Cool! I've always wanted to see the lake."

The gate creaks even louder as we go through it. You'd think, if there were someone inside, they'd call out now, to see who was coming in.

But no one does. The only sound is from a pair of gray squirrels racing each other up the trunk of a silver birch, playing happily in the leafless branches, their tails waving like soft furry fans as they dart, light as birds, from one twig to another.

"Wow." Taylor pauses to stare at the expanse of water, fringed by oak trees and weeping willows. "It's beautiful."

"You should see it in summer," I say. "I hope my grandmother gets the fountain going again."

The fountain, in the center of the lake, is a gigantic marble confection, dolphins leaping out toward the water, their smiling mouths open. When the pumps are turned on, water springs from them in high jets that curve through the sky like the arching bodies of the dolphins themselves. It's really beautiful and exhilarating to see.

But I can't help but feel a little sad when I look out around the water. The bare branches of the oak trees, the weeping willows trailing in the water, and the empty fountain at the center . . . sometimes I think there's nothing more poignant than a fountain that's been turned off so long you can't remember the last time it had water tumbling through it.

"There are little boats in there," I tell Taylor, pointing to the small boathouse on the far side of the lake, built of the same gray stone as the low balustrade that borders the water. "My dad used to take me out in one."

"Nice," Taylor says, starting to stroll toward it.

I step up onto the balustrade and stare down into the water, which is dark with leaves floating in it. It's time for Jase or his dad to fish them out, rake them into mulch. And that makes me wonder again why the gate was open. I don't see a single tool lying around, nothing that would indicate that there's a Barnes here about to get to work. There are old wheelbarrow tracks in the muddy grass, but the boathouse, which contains gardening tools as well as the boats, is padlocked securely. I can see the lock from here, hanging in an unbroken loop, holding the double doors together. There isn't so much as a rake leaning against the side, ready to be used on the leaves scattered beneath the trees.

Something's very wrong here. My nerve endings are tingling. All my physical alarm systems are going off. I'm shivering, and not just from the cold air on my sweaty skin.

"Taylor," I call, "we should probably get going."

Taylor is over by the boathouse, staring at a weeping willow whose heavy branches are dipping into the water, thickly clustered. I realize why that tree has attracted Taylor's attention. Looking at it, you can see that the branches have formed a weird shape where they brush against the ground. Almost as if there's someone lying underneath them, with one hand out, trailing in the water . . .

"Scarlett," Taylor says in a small, tight voice. "You should come over and have a look at this."

Suddenly, I'm sprinting across the grass, my trainers slipping on wet leaves, jumping over dark patches that will send me flying, around the perimeter of the lake, past Taylor, who is still standing by the boathouse.

Pleasedon'tbeJase, I'm thinking frantically, *pleasedon't beJase. . . .*

But the hand is white. I see that as I get closer. Though not white in a literal sense; it's actually bluish gray and blotchy. Old-looking, its knuckles big and swollen, sticking out of a tattered corduroy jacket cuff that's so frayed some threads are coming loose and dangling down into the grass.

I'm on my knees now, by the person lying under the weeping willow, reaching for the hand. It's ice-cold to the touch. I pull the branches away, exposing the rest of the body, which is lying on its side.

I don't need to try to feel for a pulse. It's obvious from the glassy eyes, the livid, blotchy skin, the darkness at the jawline, where blood has started to collect, that Mr. Barnes is dead.

86

nine

A HUNDRED STUFFED PENGUINS
OF VARYING SIZES

I can't breathe. I can't breathe. I'm seeing dots before my eyes and my vision's blurring. I think I'm going to throw up or pass out or both.

"Head down," Taylor says, shoving my head in between my knees and holding me steady, one hand on my head, the other on my shoulders, making sure I don't fall. "Breathe with me, okay? In . . . out . . . slower . . . in . . . out . . ."

I've never felt this dizzy in my life. Thank God I was already close to the ground. If I'd been standing, I'm sure my knees would have buckled under me.

"Take it easy. . . . In . . . out . . . in . . . out . . ."

Taylor's voice and clasp are incredibly reassuring. There's no one I'd rather have with me in a crisis, not even Jase. Taylor has the coolest head on her shoulders of anyone I know. She's rock steady, one of the rare people who get even more calm and focused in an emergency.

And I should know. Last year, Taylor and I had to deal

with someone trying to kill us both, someone who nearly got away with it.

Ugh. Dead bodies. All the dead bodies I've seen in my short life. Three in the space of a year. What's *wrong* with me? I swear, I thought I'd never have to see a corpse ever again, and Mr. Barnes's was particularly bad. Though my eyes are closed, I can see the color and texture of his skin, grayish, spongy, and bloodless, and another surge of vomit threatens to burst up at the back of my throat. I can taste it, sour and burning and acid.

Tears form in my eyes and start flowing down my cheeks. It actually feels as if my body's trying to cleanse me of the unbearable pain and shock I'm feeling.

I start to sob, quietly, but Taylor hears it and murmurs, "Good, Scarlett . . . let it out," rubbing my shoulders with one palm, still holding me steady.

I'm crying louder now, bawling, really, my face dripping with liquid. And that's another reason I'd rather have Taylor with me in a crisis than anyone else. We've been through so much together already that I couldn't care less if she sees me like this, snotty, wet, my eyes swollen from crying.

Eventually, I can't weep any more. My sobs turn to deep, heaving gulps as I draw in air, and Taylor guides me to sit back, my legs folding in front of me. I grasp my knees, managing to hold myself up, and wipe my face with the sleeve of my sweatshirt, which quickly gets sodden and sloppy with tears and snot.

"It's Jase's dad, isn't it?" Taylor says from her kneeling position next to me.

I manage a nod.

"Oh, *shit.*"

I nod again. Taylor gets up, leans over the low balustrade beside her, and scoops up some water in her cupped hands, patting it over my face. It's cold and refreshing and it helps to calm me down. She goes back for another handful, and this time she dabs it on the back of my neck and my wrists. Weirdly, this helps even more. I hear my breathing slowing, becoming more regular.

"Scarlett, I'm not going to ask if you're okay," Taylor says, her voice softer than I've ever heard it. "Because there's no way you could possibly be okay. But someone needs to go and tell your grandmother so she can call the cops, and you're in no state to do anything like that. So whenever you're ready, I'm going to go off and leave you here, just till I can get to your grandmother, and then I'll come right back. I'm going to close the gate behind me, so I doubt anyone'll try to come in, but someone should stay here, just to be on the safe side."

I draw in a deep gulp of air.

"It's okay. You should go," I say. "I'll be . . ."

She's right. I can't say I'm fine.

"I can wait till you get back," I finish instead.

Taylor stands up, staring down at the body.

"Look at that." She points to something half concealed beneath Mr. Barnes, under a flap of his open jacket. "You think he came out here for a drink and tripped over?"

It's an empty whisky bottle. I don't know anything about whisky. None of the girls I know drinks anything but vodka, or champagne and white wine. Clear, girlie drinks. Whisky

89

seems really hard-core to me. But as far as I can remember, it's the same brand I saw Mr. Barnes drinking from last night. The bright yellow label looks very familiar.

"More than likely," I say to her, but I have my doubts.

"You sure you're okay waiting?" she asks.

I nod once more.

Taylor doesn't ask me again, she just goes, sprinting away as fast as if the hounds of hell are after her. And I turn my head to stare down at Jase's father's body, finally feeling ready to survey it.

It looks as if he tripped and fell and hit his head on the stone balustrade. There's a long bruise across his face, a horrible dark purple stripe, and when I look at the hand that's stretched out on the grass, I notice that it's at a weird angle, as if it got broken when he fell over and tried to catch himself. I lift some branches off the lower part of his body, and see that it looks like there's blood on his trouser leg, seeped through. Although it's disgusting, I grit my teeth and hook up the dirty old fabric of the trousers, driven by a need to investigate that I don't even fully understand.

There are two long welts about halfway up Mr. Barnes's calf. The welts bled, because the hairs on his skin are coated in dried blood, matted down, and I wonder if he hit himself on the balustrade, staggering around, before he fell.

I speculate about how long he's been lying out here. I can't see him leaving the cozy warm house last night, the comfort of his saggy armchair and TV, to unlock the gate to the lake and roam around in the dark with a bottle of whisky. It doesn't make sense.

So he must have come here—what, this morning? Still

drinking? But why didn't he lock the gate behind him? And has anyone missed him yet?

An awful thought dawns on me. I'm amazed it didn't hit me before. Shock is a really strange phenomenon. It can drive all the normal reactions you'd think you'd have straight out of your head for much longer than you'd expect.

Jase. I'm going to have to tell Jase that his dad is dead.

And that's immediately followed by an even worse thought.

Maybe he'll actually be grateful.

. . .

"Did you touch the body at all?" the police officer is asking me.

"Just to see if he was alive," I say.

Great, Scarlett. The first thing you say to the police, and it's a lie. Nice way to start.

But I don't think they'd be that keen on the fact that I checked to see where that blood came from on Mr. Barnes's leg.

"He was *definitely* dead," Taylor chimes in.

Detective Sergeant Landon's eyebrows shoot up as she looks at Taylor.

"You sound very sure," she comments.

"He was stone cold," Taylor says simply.

DS Landon glances over at my grandmother, who's as poised as ever, sitting on a straight-backed armchair, her hands folded in her lap. She meets DS Landon's eyes with not an iota of change in her calm expression, her blue eyes clear. I've never seen anything faze my grandmother, and I can't imagine what would. Her white hair is drawn into a bob, the ends tucked neatly behind her ears. The cardigan of her pale peach twinset is neatly buttoned and turned back at the neck to display her pearl necklace; her tweed skirt is smoothed over her knees; her back is poker straight.

Wherever my grandmother is, she's always the still, calm focus. Her authority is so impressive that she never even needs to raise her voice to silence everyone else.

"Taylor," my grandmother pronounces, "is a singularly level-headed girl."

Taylor looks simultaneously flattered and amazed.

"And you didn't see anything unusual about the body?" DS Landon asks me.

"He had a big mark on his face, like he'd fallen and hit it," I reply. "And there was the whisky bottle under him. Taylor and I both saw it."

"*Whisky bottle?*" my grandmother says in a tone so icy that we all shiver.

I nod.

"Empty," I add.

I'm trying to keep calm. My leg wants to jiggle nervously, and in my heightened emotional state, I watch my kneecap bouncing up and down and actually reach out a hand as sur-reptitiously as I can, holding it so it can't move.

Only then, the other leg starts to jiggle. I can't hold that one too. It would look crazy, and even if I tried, something else would probably start to jerk around next and then I really would look like I have a motor neuron disorder.

I try to lock my legs into place, heels clamped on the

ground, quads holding them down. Okay, everyone will expect me to be a bit worked up; I just found a dead body, after all. But Taylor is as calm and poised as ever, so if I look like a neurotic mess beside her that'll be suspicious, and might direct the police's attention to me. The last thing I want in my life is any more police attention, especially with Jase so closely involved in all of this.

Besides, my grandmother is giving me a very cool, disapproving look. Wakefields remain composed and controlled under all circumstances. Wakefields do not show an excess of emotion. Wakefields behave better than anyone around them, to set the best example possible.

I think of the "Wakefield Hall Etiquette Guide for Students" and have to stifle a laugh as it suddenly occurs to me that Lady Wakefield omitted to have me pose for a photograph in it demonstrating how to react when your boyfriend's father is dead under mysterious circumstances and you find the body. The laugh keeps rising; oh God, I'm getting hysterical. I pinch myself so hard I nearly draw blood, but at least it kills any impulse I have to burst into a giggling fit.

My grandmother tuts her tongue very loudly indeed, but whether it's at the whisky bottle revelation or my inability to control my physical reflexes, I have no idea. Probably both.

"Has anyone informed his poor son, Detective?" she asks DS Landon.

"That's Jason Barnes, correct?" DS Landon flicks through her notepad. "His grandmother's informed us that he went out after breakfast and hasn't come back yet, Lady Wakefield."

"Someone should ring him," my grandmother says firmly.

93

"We don't seem to have a mobile number for him," DS Landon says. "His grandmother says he has one, but she doesn't know the number."

"Scarlett has it," Taylor blurts out.

Everyone looks at me. We're sitting round an inlaid marquetry coffee table, on chairs upholstered in a pale green silk and caught with tiny covered buttons, which are incredibly uncomfortable to sit on; I shift as a button cuts into my leg, and my grandmother shoots me a swift icy glance of reproach for not sitting up straight.

The chairs are arranged in a semicircle. It's the meet-and-greet-the-parents area of my grandmother's study, by the bow window that looks over the wide expanse of paved terraces below, where most girls gather to play games and hang out in school breaks. I'm sure my grandmother has carefully chosen this room as her headquarters because of the unrivaled surveillance opportunities it offers.

I never know how far her surveillance skills extend, or whether it's simply that she has so much self-control she never looks surprised, but she doesn't seem remotely taken aback at the revelation that I am close enough to Jase to have his mobile phone number.

"They're friends," Taylor adds, her voice bland, but she ducks her head and directs a hard stare at me. I think she's telling me to say something, to look natural, but that's so far beyond my capabilities at this precise moment that all I can do is nod in agreement.

"They've known each other for years," my grandmother adds in a deliberately careless tone to Sergeant Landon.

"After all, they're the only two children who live at Wakefield Hall all year round."

This isn't true. I never met Jase till last year, and I suspect she knows that. I clear my throat and manage to say:

"My phone's in my locker. I could go and get it now, if you'd like."

I'm addressing Sergeant Landon, but I'm looking at my grandmother, into her bright blue eyes, trying to work out how much she knows. It's always a mistake to underestimate her.

"That's a school rule," my grandmother informs the sergeant. "The girls are not allowed to carry mobiles on their persons, even switched off."

"Very sensible," Sergeant Langdon agrees, even as I think:

And you've been with me the whole time since Taylor brought the police back to Mr. Barnes's body. I haven't had a chance to get to my locker and ring Jase. If I hadn't been so much of an idiot, I would have told Taylor to bring my phone, but I wasn't thinking straight.

"Sergeant Landon, why don't you take Scarlett to her locker and locate her telephone?" my grandmother suggests.

Her expression is completely unreadable, her smile bland and polite, a facade behind which all her thoughts are concealed. If she's cross with Taylor and me for trespassing by going into the lake enclosure, if she knows more than she's saying about how close I am to Jase, I can't read any of it on her face.

"And then, Scarlett, take Taylor and go to your aunt's,"

my grandmother instructs. "You certainly won't be fit for classes for the rest of the day, either of you. I think the police should be given a chance to locate poor Jason Barnes before the story of his unfortunate father spreads all around school." She fixes us with a basilisk stare. "You will of course not mention a word of this to any of your fellow students until you are told by me that you are allowed to do so."

We stand up and DS Landon shakes my grandmother's hand.

"Thank you for your help, Lady Wakefield," she says deferentially.

"Please tell poor Mrs. Barnes that I will visit her later today," my grandmother says, and instead of telling her that the police aren't a message delivery service, DS Landon nods politely and turns to leave the room.

Wow. My grandmother could probably shoot someone in the face with a shotgun in the middle of Wakefield village and all the police would do is make her a cup of tea, tell her they're sure she had a very good reason for doing it, and send her back to Wakefield Hall again.

I can't help admiring Lady Wakefield's perfect composure. But sometimes it's so cold that it's positively glacial. I know that's what she wants me to aspire to, that same level of supreme poise, where the most you allow yourself is a raise of the eyebrow or a tut of the lips on hearing the worst news imaginable.

The thing is, I don't think that's me. No, I *know* that's not me. And I don't want her to try to turn me into a clone of her. I don't want to end up the kind of person who doesn't even give her granddaughter a hug and ask how she is after she's seen a second corpse in under a year.

As we walk down the corridor, still in the old part of the Hall, the polished boards smelling lightly of wax, I have a flash of memory: being carried down here by my mother. She held me close to her chest, looking over her shoulder at the receding door to my grandmother's rooms. Winter sunlight on the glass of the oil paintings hanging on the paneled walls, faded Turkish carpet runners on the floor, my mother's scent all around me, her arms holding me tight.

I so wish my parents were still alive.

We cross over into the new wing, concrete and white-painted walls, the contrast stark and immediate. The school corridors are empty and echoing. Everyone else is back in afternoon classes, and I doubt any of the girls have the faintest idea what's just happened.

We clatter downstairs to the changing rooms and locker area, which always reeks of smelly trainers and gym clothes, a lingering odor of underarms and feet so ingrained into the walls and floor that even in the school holidays, it never completely fades. I fish my phone out of my locker and pull up Jase's number for DS Landon to copy onto hers.

"Anything else you can think of, here's my card," she says, handing it to me as she dials Jase's number.

I take ages slipping it into my pocket, my heart pounding. His phone must have gone to voice mail, because DS Landon is leaving a message telling him to ring her as a matter of urgency. My fingers are already dancing across my phone keys as I turn away, texting him to ring me ASAP.

"If you see Jase, tell him to ring me soonest, okay, Scarlett?" DS Landon calls over her shoulder as she walks away, and I nod virtuously and probably unconvincingly.

"Are you all right?" Taylor asks.

"I don't know," I say. I've just rung Jase's number, but he isn't answering. I hang up as it goes to voice mail, unsure about what to say to him in a message. All I want is to be able to break the news to Jase, and to make sure he's okay before he goes to the police.

"Hey," Taylor says, trying to lighten the mood, "at least we get to watch crappy afternoon TV, right?"

But when we get to Aunt Gwen's, turning on the TV is the last thing on Taylor's mind. She wanders round the living room, eyes wide, picking up every single china object one by one in awe and wonder.

"Wow," she says eventually. "I didn't know there were this many penguins in the world."

"You haven't even looked at the ones on the sofa yet," I say, sinking down among them.

I'm not officially banned from using Aunt Gwen's living room, it's just that she's usually in it, not having much of a life, and the last thing either of us wants is to spend any social time together. So apart from when I'm showering or grabbing a soft drink from the fridge, I'm pretty much always in my bedroom. I have a TV in there and I watch a lot of stuff on the computer, but I must admit that actually sitting on a proper sofa is very nice.

I too am gobsmacked by the sheer extent of the penguin collection; I haven't been in here for quite a while and it's as if they've been breeding since then. The china ones are now covering every available surface, and the sofa is so clustered with stuffed penguins that I'm sitting on at least four of them, with a further penguin head sticking over my shoulder as if it's trying to watch TV with me.

Taylor turns to look at me and executes such a perfect double-take that I crack up laughing, and keep on much longer than her expression warrants. But I'm so grateful for something to laugh at that I actually can't stop for quite a while.

"I feel like we're on Antarctica," she says, plopping down next to me, dislodging several more penguins as she does so. "We just need a polar bear for the finishing touch."

"Her tea set's all penguins too," I confess. "And there are lots of coffee mugs."

"I just bet there are," Taylor says, reaching for the remote. "Remind me not to go into the kitchen cupboards. I might actually have a meltdown."

I look at her. Neither of us has had a chance to shower since our run; we're both a bit sticky, sweat stains drying on our T-shirts. But I don't want to take my clothes off yet. It would feel too vulnerable to be naked right now, with the water pouring down on me. I just want to curl up into a ball on the sofa, with Taylor. And about a hundred stuffed penguins of varying sizes.

"Hey, let's find the people with the biggest problems on TV. That's always the best thing for cheering you up." Taylor clicks on the television. "Some juicy lie-detector tests and people cheating with dwarves and stuff. Cool. I never get to watch this at the dorm."

I don't think anything will successfully distract me from

the fact that my phone feels like it's burning a hole in my pocket.

But Taylor's right, as she usually is. The sight of a lot of larger-than-life people bouncing up and down on their chairs, screaming at each other and sobbing hysterically as they watch their partners making out with sexy decoys in the greenroom of the TV studio, is hypnotically compelling. I manage so successfully to lose myself in their over-the-top stories that when my phone finally rings, I jump in shock.

It's Jase.

"Scarlett?" he says in a low voice. "What's going on? I've got these texts from you, and some voice mails from the *police*—"

"Where are you?" I interrupt. I can't tell him over the phone. I just can't.

"At the main gates. The messages from the coppers freaked me out, so I rode up the main road and pulled the bike into the bushes, so they won't see it. I was hoping you could get out of school or something, and meet me."

"Taylor and I are here at Aunt Gwen's," I say, jumping up. "Come here, I'll tell you everything when I see you."

"I can't come there," Jase's voice rises. "Your aunt—"

"It's okay, she won't be back for at least an hour," I say swiftly.

There's silence at the other end of the line.

"Jase?" I say, looking at the phone, thinking that maybe we got cut off for some reason. But no, the line's still active.

"Jase?" I say again.

No reply. I start to panic. Did the police just find him at the gates? I run over to the window. We're practically next to them; the gatekeeper's cottage was built so that he, or one of his family, could nip out and swing open the imposing iron gates, curlicued with the Wakefield crest, whenever a carriage needed to pass through. I press my face to the glass, but mostly I see the oak trees that surround the cottage, and beyond them, in glimpses, the iron fence that runs round the perimeter of the Wakefield Hall grounds.

The doorbell rings. I scream, jump, and dash across the room.

"Honestly, you're worse than the people on *Jerry Springer*," Taylor drawls, watching a woman the size of a house beating a man the size of the house, naked but for a tie and his boxer shorts, over the head with a wedding bouquet.

"*Jase!*" I pull the door open and fall into his arms.

His leather jacket creaks as he wraps his arms around me, his chin coming down on the top of my head. I know it's irrational to think that nothing bad can happen to me when Jase is around. I know Jase can't protect me from all the hurt and pain in the world outside.

But right now, for a few moments, that's exactly what it feels like.

Sometimes an illusion can be really comforting.

I pull my head back from his chest, looking up into his handsome face. His lips are drawn together and his eyes are more dark bronze than gold. Even the color seems to have drained from his skin, which has an ashy tinge instead of being its usually healthy pale cappuccino.

"Oh my God," I whisper. "You already know."

101

Ten

"I WISHED THAT HE WAS DEAD"

I scan Jase, trying to pick up any clues I can.

"How did you find out?" I ask him.

He sighs, hugging me closer to him again. "My gran rang me."

"But she told the police she didn't have your number," I say.

He laughs dryly. "My gran doesn't tell the coppers anything they don't know already. Nor did my dad, as a matter of principle."

Suddenly, he pulls back, looking down into my face, his expression concerned.

"How did you find out?"

I swallow hard. "Taylor and I found him near the lake."

"Hey, Jase," Taylor says from the sofa.

"Hey," he says distractedly to her, still looking down at me. "So what happened?"

"We were jogging past the lake and saw the gate wasn't

locked, which seemed weird, so we went inside to see if anything was wrong. Taylor spotted your dad, lying down under a weeping willow."

Jase smooths the hair from my face, not seeming to mind that it's frizzed-up from my run earlier. "I'm so sorry, Scarlett."

I take his hand and pull him inside, meaning to take him up to my room.

"Nuh-uh," says Taylor from the sofa. "Bad idea. What if your aunt comes back? You'll really be in trouble then."

I glance over at the wall clock, whose little swinging wooden pendulum is—you guessed it—carved in the shape of a penguin.

"It's an hour before last-lesson bell," I say. "She can't get back here till then."

"Oh yeah?" Taylor says grimly. "What if she hasn't got a class scheduled, and your grandma tells her what happened to her niece, and she decides to come back here and check that we're not drinking her booze and photographing the penguins doing freaky stuff to each other?"

"Penguins?" Jase mutters in disbelief. He looks into the living room. "*Blimey*," he says, taking in the scene. "Hardcore."

My heart sinks; I was so looking forward to being alone with Jase in my room, curling up on the bed with him. But I know Taylor's right.

I tighten my hand around Jase's. "This is so *rubbish*. We can't even sit down and comfort each other."

"It sucks," Taylor agrees sympathetically. "Look, I'll hold down the fort here, okay? You two go off and if your aunt does show, Scarlett, I'll say you headed back to the library to get a book you need for your homework. Take your phone, so I can text you if she turns up here. Just try not to get caught, because it'll be both of our asses."

"Thanks, Taylor," Jase and I say, almost in synch.

"Just be back here by end-of-school bell," Taylor warns, settling deeper into the sofa. "Oh, and Scarlett? Come back with a library book."

. . .

"Shall we go to the maze?" Jase suggests. "We're the only people who know how to get through to the middle."

"No," I disagree. "People might see us going in. And even if they couldn't get to the center, they could still easily hear us through the hedges."

Jase nods.

"You're almost as good as Taylor."

"Almost?"

"That detail about the library book was *thorough*," he marvels.

Despite the crisis hanging over us like a huge black thundercloud, I can't help cracking a small smile. It means a lot to me that Jase appreciates Taylor.

"Yeah, it's great having her on my side," I say.

"So what bright ideas d'you have, then, since you've shot mine down?"

"The old temple," I say immediately. "It's got lots of places to hide, and we can see anyone coming."

To do him credit, Jase never gets grumpy when I have a plan that's better than his.

"Sold," he says.

At school we call it a temple, because it has that shape. But that's a nickname. Officially it's a folly. Built by a Wakefield ancestor in the early nineteeth century on a knoll that overlooks the lake and the Great Lawn, it does have the indented marble pillars and curving semicircular back wall that make you think of a Greek temple. I suspect it of being an original one, illegally bought and smuggled out of Greece. There was a lot of that going on in the early eighteen hundreds—we studied it in art history at St. Tabby's—and my grandmother, who's usually a mine of information on anything relating to the Hall, is always suspiciously quiet on the subject of the so-called folly.

Not to mention that she gets very cross whenever anyone refers to it as a temple.

If there was ever an altar here, it's long gone. Instead, there are three marble benches, placed along the curve of the back wall, so you can sit down and appreciate the vista: the lake, the green sward of lawn beyond, and the side elevation of the Hall, with its stacked terraces leading down to the lawn. I realize, as soon as we sit, that we can actually see the place where Taylor and I found Mr. Barnes.

I flinch, looking at Jase, who's staring out over the expanse of water, his expression unreadable, his arm thrown over my shoulders.

"Cold night to be out," he says finally. "Cold night to lie out there all alone."

"Do you think he went out after you left?" I ask him.

He shrugs slowly.

"Why would he? But Dad did what Dad wanted. You couldn't tell him anything."

I rest my hand on his thigh. The sky is still gray, and seems to hang very low above us oppressively, not a hint of sunlight filtering through.

"I'm sorry about not coming last night," he says. "To the barn. But you got my texts, right?"

I nod. "Eventually. But I didn't have my phone with me. So I sneaked over to your cottage to see if you were there."

"Oh, Jesus. You heard the barney? Me and Dad?"

"I saw it," I say. "I climbed the cherry tree."

Jase looks away. "Dad said a lot of stuff when he was drunk. I don't think he meant the half of it."

"Your dad isn't you, Jase. *Wasn't* you," I correct myself, sounding so heartfelt that he squeezes me even closer.

"We fought so much, Scarlett. All the time," he says, still staring ahead of him at the lake enclosure. "He was never easy. Never. When I was little I used to yell at him that I wished he was dead, and I'd get the back of his hand across my face for it. So I learned not to say it, but there are times I thought it, I'll tell you. Plenty of times. Last night, for one." His fists clench again. "What he was saying about you, and your mum—I've heard him go on about the Wakefields before, but never like that."

"Why did he hate the Wakefields so much?" I ask in a sad little voice. "Did my grandmother and he not get along?"

Jase shakes his head.

"It's as much a mystery to me as it is to you," he murmurs.

106

"I never understood any of it." Then he lets go of me, both his hands coming forward to cup his face. "But he was still my dad, you know?" he says into his palms. "I wished he was dead, but I never meant it. . . . Scarlett, I never meant it. . . ."

His voice trails off into ragged sobs. His shoulders start to heave.

Jase is crying in front of me.

It's almost frightening, Jase breaking down like this. He's so strong: strong enough to stand up to his dad for me, to ride a powerful motorbike, to dig ditches, to prune trees with a chain saw. I didn't realize how much I relied on that strength until I see him hunched over, vulnerable, crying his heart out.

Physical strength is different from emotional strength, I tell myself firmly. *Just because Jase is strong, that doesn't mean he can't cry when he needs to.*

And it also means he really trusts you. Because he wouldn't let himself go like this around anyone but you.

Tentatively, I slip an arm round him, cuddling up to him as close as I can, and he doesn't push me away. In fact, he turns to me, his face damp, reaching out for me, and I scooch up even closer, picking up my legs and swinging them over his so I'm sitting partly in his lap and he's burying his face in my chest, still crying. I stroke his short dark curly hair.

"I love you," I whisper into his hair, so faintly I'm sure he can't hear me. But it's a huge release just to have said the words to him, and I feel a sense of calm flood through me as I sit there, holding him, hearing him quiet down, too.

His breath becomes more even. Eventually, he raises his head, wiping his eyes on the ribbed wristband of his jacket, swallowing hard. He looks at me, such sadness in his eyes that it breaks my heart.

And then our lips meet, his very soft and full and tasting delicately of salt from his tears. I close my eyes and melt into him completely.

"What a *lovely*, touching scene," comes an all-too-familiar mocking voice. "Careful, Scarlett! You'll make your girlfriend jealous."

eleven

KISS OF DEATH GIRL

Plum is smoking a cigarette, her long chestnut hair falling down her back, a slim black overcoat belted tightly around her waist with a wide strip of patent leather. She looks fabulously glamorous, like a femme fatale from a French film. All that's missing is a fog machine for extra atmosphere. Still, the pale trail of smoke, curling upward around her, adds an extra touch of sophistication.

"You *are* a busy girl, Scarlett," Plum says, smiling evilly. "I never saw any hint of this at St. Tabby's. You were always hanging around with those two little friends of yours. We all thought you were gay for each other. Terribly sweet."

I jump off Jase's lap and stand in front of him, my hands on my hips, shielding him from her sight.

"From what everyone tells me, you and Taylor got together the moment you came to Wakefield Hall," Plum says, strolling toward me, her glossy knee-high leather boots definitely not approved school wear. "It's lucky Jase isn't the jealous type, isn't it?"

I see her staring closely at me, her long, slanting green

eyes narrowing as she assesses the effect she's having. I hear Jase's motorcycle boots shift in the gravel. I doubt he likes what he's hearing, but I appreciate the fact that he's letting me fight my own battles.

Then again, maybe he's just too grief-stricken to say anything.

Plum raises her eyebrows and takes a long drag at her cigarette, sensing an opportunity to strike hard.

"Though you did get around a bit in your blaze of glory at St. Tabby's, didn't you? Short, but *packed* with incidents." Plum looks past me, at Jase, who I devoutly hope by now has managed to pull himself together a bit, so that Plum can't spot signs of his tears and use them against him. "She told you all about her last few days at St. Tabby's, didn't she, Jase? But you two are *so* close, I'm sure you tell each other absolutely *everything*."

Now she's got me. I've tensed up from head to toe. My body feels like one tight coiled wire, about to explode.

"Oh dear. Don't tell me you kept mum about it?" Plum says, with her special little pointy smile, where her lips don't curve so much as strike upward at the corners so her mouth is shaped like a V. "Oh dear. Don't tell me you *haven't* told Jase about your rather lurid past? Two boys competing for your attention, and only one survivor! *Terribly* dramatic, but just a little bit frightening for anyone who wants to follow in those footsteps, I would imagine."

Behind her, two crows sweep by, cawing loudly to each other, the flap of their wings heavy in the still air. They're loud enough that even Plum reacts, turning her head to

110

watch their flight. I can see how someone could read the appearance of the big black birds as ominous, but strangely, they remind me that there's a reality beyond this moment, this confrontation with Plum in an ancient stone temple, with Jase sitting behind me, a silent spectator whom Plum keeps attempting to drag into the action.

The crows have given me respite for a couple of vital moments, with Plum's eyes off me. Long enough for me to summon up my resolve and decide to go on the attack. There's only one thing to do in a situation like this: call her bluff.

So that's exactly what I do.

"You know what, Plum?" I say, sitting back down next to Jase, removing myself from the eyeball-to-eyeball staring match, hoping this makes me look more confident. "Jase and I have been so busy with other things that I haven't had time yet to mention that to him. Why don't *you* go ahead and fill in all the gaps in my CV that you think he ought to know? Out of the goodness of your heart, of course!"

Nice, I think, my heart surging as I see her eyes narrow in anger. *Well played, Scarlett. Now she'll look like a telltale if she tries to say anything to Jase.*

Jase stretches out his hand to me, and I take it. I don't dare to look at him, though, because I have to focus all my concentration on Plum. She's much more expert at this game than I am. She's played it every day for years and years, while I floated in a bubble of nonsnarky, noncompetitive friendship. Silly me! What was I thinking?

"Oh, I'll leave it to you to tell him all the sordid details," she says eventually, doing a throwaway gesture with her cigarette that indicates that kind of thing is very far beneath her. "But let's just say that you don't get a nickname like the Kiss of Death Girl for nothing, do you?"

The leather of his jacket creaks lightly as Jase turns his head to look at me.

"I read about that in the papers," he says, his forehead creasing in an effort of memory. "Last year, wasn't it?"

"Yes," I say, swallowing hard. "Last summer. I'll tell you all about it later. It wasn't my fault."

A boy called Dan McAndrew dropped down dead at my feet after kissing me, my first-ever kiss. So I had to go on what amounted to a quest to find out the truth of what had happened. It was the hardest thing I ever had to do in my life, but at least it gave me the answers I was desperate to find, and allows me, now, to hold my head high and say those four words: *It wasn't my fault.*

God, that feels wonderful.

Plum drops her cigarette to the ground and crushes it with a practiced twist of her heel.

"So the ambulance we saw earlier, and the police cars," she prattles on. "Before I sneaked out here for a fag, they told us some staff member had had an accident, and I just thought one of those *noxious* cooks had sliced off their hand in the meat grinder and they'd tried to feed it to us in that ghastly chili or something. But it's more than that, isn't it?'

Her stare on me is like acid on an etching plate, cutting through to the truth of the situation. I open my mouth to deflect her, but I'm not fast enough.

"Someone *died*, didn't they?" she breathes, her eyes gleaming with an unholy light of satisfaction. "And you're

112

involved in it some way, otherwise there's no way you'd be out of class. *Talk* about Kiss of Death! What on earth is *wrong* with you?"

I've been doing so well. Really, I have. Not responding to extreme provocation. Actually removing myself from the field of conflict. But now Plum's hit the target, gone for gold. She's triggered all the memories of her and her set at St. Tabby's, whispering "Kiss of Death" at me in the corridor, ostentatiously pulling their clothes away from any contact from me, pretending that I might contaminate them with some deadly infection.

And even worse, she's made a connection between Dan's death and Jase's father's, planting in Jase's mind, perhaps, the idea that I really am cursed in some way. That the deaths that happen around me *are*, after all, somehow my fault . . .

I'm on my feet and hurtling toward her so fast she doesn't register my approach till I'm right up in her face. *That's the thing about taking on someone who's used to sprinting like a demon to get up enough kinetic energy to do two handsprings plus a front tuck somersault*, I think vindictively as I reach her.

Plum may be the world champion at winding people up, but she's so confident about her skills, she forgets I've got a few of my own.

She doesn't flinch at first. She just takes another cigarette out of a silver case and puts it in her mouth. I pluck it from her lips and chuck it on the ground.

"That's a *filthy* habit," I hiss at her. "It's as disgusting as you are."

As twin spots of red flare with anger on her cheeks, Plum raises her hand to slap me. And as soon as it gets physical,

113

she's in my territory, not her own. Not that I'm used to fist-fighting. I haven't been in a proper fight in my life. But my reflexes are great. I have fast-twitch muscles, which contract really, really swiftly, and I catch her wrist with my left hand as it comes toward me and push her arm down, away from our bodies, holding it there with ease, my fingers biting into her wrist bones.

Without conscious intention, my right arm flies up. She shrinks back, her other hand coming up to protect her face, but I knock it away so hard she'd have spun around if I hadn't still been holding her wrist.

Her face is terrified, all color drained from it. Her green eyes are wide, her mouth open in an O of shock and fear. Finally, *finally*, Plum is as scared of me as I am of her. And honestly, I swear, I want to hit her with everything I have, and feel justified in doing it, because she started it, she started *every single fight we ever had*, and this punch has been coming to her a long, long time—

"Scarlett! Stop!"

I can't see Plum's white mask of terror any longer. Jase has shouldered between us, grabbing me and breaking my grip on Plum, bringing my arms up and crossing them over my chest, holding them tightly.

"Scarlett, stop!" he yells at me again, as instinctively I wrestle to be free of him. "She's not worth it!"

I take a breath to say something, but Jase is turning his head, shouting at Plum.

"Get out of here, now! We've had about enough of you bitching at us. That's my *father* they took out of here in an ambulance this morning, I'll have you know! And Scarlett *found* him. Can you *imagine* what kind of state we're in, you cow? Sod off and leave us alone!"

Plum shrinks back, looking genuinely shocked at the realization that she's been taunting us over the death of someone so closely related. Her lips part, as if she's about to say something.

I wait. Maybe Plum will drill down into whatever tiny reserve of human feeling she's got left under that facade of ice, and do the decent thing: apologize.

I twist around Jase enough to fix my eyes on Plum. Her gaze is lowered. She looks almost contrite.

And then she shoves her chin up high in the air, defiantly, and turns away without another word.

She tosses her mane of hair back and stalks off, her heels pounding the stone, the skirt of her coat swishing from side to side as furiously as a cat thrashing its tail.

"Good riddance to bad rubbish," Jase mutters. "You okay now? Can I let you go without you smacking me in the face?"

I nod gruffly as he releases his grip on my forearms.

"She just keeps digging till she gets to you," I mumble furiously. "I didn't really *want* to hit her, but she was going to slap me first and—"

"It's okay, Scarlett. I don't think you're some sort of violent psycho, I promise," he says, hugging me. "My dad used to say all kinds of stuff, but that girl could make a nun so angry she'd brain her with a crucifix."

I giggle weakly, my nose squished against his chest. But deep down, I'm in a spin of insecurity. Plum's words have cut me very deeply. Dan's death wasn't my fault. I do know that. But is there something about me that means people keep

115

dying around me? Am I the Kiss of Death Girl after all, only not in a literal sense?

"You can tell me all about your past whenever you're ready," Jase says, hugging me even tighter. "But don't worry, I won't rush you. I've got secrets enough of my own."

Oh God, I think, clinging to Jase in the cold winter air. *I can't deal with anything more. I don't want to know.*

Twelve

WITHER AND PERISH

"There is one more announcement today," my grandmother says, a diminutive figure behind the huge carved lectern on the stage of the assembly hall. Even without a microphone of any sort, her voice carries effortlessly right to the very back row, where the Upper Sixth sit.

We don't see that much of the Upper Sixth around school; they all have a fanatic gleam in their eyes. They're constantly studying to ensure they get As in every single A- and S-Level they take, so they can swan into Oxford and Cambridge and the London School of Economics. Their parents pay large sums of money to get their daughters on the Wakefield Hall conveyor belt, which sweeps its best and brightest to the most prestigious universities in the country, but at this school no one takes anything for granted.

"Some of you may have noticed that an ambulance was called to school yesterday, and that it was attended by police vehicles," Lady Wakefield continues, her aristocratic, old-fashioned accent giving the last word three long syllables: it comes out as *vee-hih-culls*. "I have no doubt that this has occasioned some speculation among you. Sadly, Kevin Barnes, our long-serving head gardener, suffered a fatal accident yesterday morning. It is a tragedy to everyone at the Hall, and we can best show our respect by discussing this as little as possible to minimize the distress to his family."

She pauses for a moment.

"For government-mandated health and safety reasons," she adds airily, "it is possible that the police may find it necessary to circulate the grounds and ensure that all the proper regulations are being observed. This is perfectly standard procedure when an accident occurs, and they may not even find it necessary to talk to any of you girls. Please do not impede them in the performance of their duties."

She turns over a piece of paper on her lectern, signaling that this subject is now closed.

"And now, our final hymn, number fifty-six. Mrs. Patel?"

The organist, invisible to us, seated high up in the organ loft, brings her hands down on the keys and her feet on the pedals in unison for the first crashing chords that introduce the hymn and give us all time to riffle through our hymnals for the correct page. The Hall reverberates with the resonance of the organ pipes as hundreds of girls shuffle back their chairs, rise to their feet, hymnals in hands, and open their mouths to sing:

Immortal, invisible, God only wise
In light inaccessible, hid from our eyes . . .

This has always been one of my favorite hymns, partly because it has such a lovely tune, uplifting and rousing. And it's fun to sing, because the notes jump all over the place and you have to concentrate to hit them all. I'm almost enjoying myself, till we come to the words:

We blossom and flourish as leaves on the tree
And wither, and perish—but naught changeth Thee.

And then I go very quiet. I can't sing the rest, I just move my lips to the music. Taylor, beside me, notices at once, because she never sings herself. She says she's so tone-deaf that her drone would frighten the little girls. The verse is over, though, and she doesn't realize why I've fallen silent.

And wither, and perish—

I shiver, thinking of Mr. Barnes's dead body beneath the tree.

The hymn is over. We're sliding the red-leather-bound hymnals into their slots on the back of the wooden chairs in front of us and filing out of the Hall. There are fifteen minutes before the first lesson starts, and Lizzie Livermore is on me like a rash immediately, her eyes wide and shiny, asking:

"Is it *true*? Is Jase's dad really dead?"

"Remember what my gran—I mean, *Lady Wakefield*—said about discussing it as little as possible?" I'm not sure I can blame Lizzie for gossiping. After all, the best way to ensure teenage girls will talk about something is to tell them not to.

"Is Jase *okay*? Plum was talking about it yesterday, but it just seemed so *ridiculous*. I mean, a death at *school*?" Lizzie babbles. "This is *Wakefield*, nothing happens here, *ever*!"

Feel free to swap lives with me for a couple of days, I think dryly. *That'll change your mind fast enough.*

"I heard you found the body, but that *can't* be true, can it?" Lizzie carries on. "That would just be *so*, I don't know, *unbelievable!*"

I can barely believe it either.

"And after—*you* know—that *thing* when you left St. Tabby's—" Lizzie knows all about Dan's death and the Kiss of Death Girl nickname. But Lizzie is very easily cowed, and her fear of my grandmother is all-encompassing; she knows not to breathe a word of it to any girl at Wakefield Hall.

She nudges me, her wrist jangling with the beaded bracelets she's copied from Plum. "I don't know how you deal with all this *death* and stuff," she breathes.

Suddenly, Taylor is upon us and staring hard at Lizzie. "Exactly," she says, "which is why Scarlett doesn't need any more gossip spreading about her. Got that?"

Lizzie visibly wilts under Taylor's gaze, like a flower dying in a vase in a speeded-up motion sequence. Her backbone seems to dissolve as she shrinks a couple of inches. Taylor cracks her knuckles, making her point very clear.

"I *haven't* been, Taylor, honestly," Lizzie says fervently.

Taylor nods in approval and Lizzie straightens up a little, smiling submissively at my best friend.

Lizzie really just wants someone to tell her what to do all the time, I reflect. *She's like a little poodle.*

"Careful, Lizzie," drawls Plum, and Lizzie's head snaps round immediately, hearing her mistress's voice. "You're not talking about the Thing We're Not Supposed to Talk

About, are you? Scarlett's pet butch will bite your head off if you do."

Plum's entourage of girls giggle dutifully at the way Plum has put capital letters onto her words for sarcastic emphasis. Plum strolls up, wearing a long belted sweater-dress that her tall, thin frame carries off very well. But just behind her is Susan, even taller and skinnier, wearing pretty much the same outfit, and though Plum looks great, Susan looks like a model. Now that she's taken to pulling her blond hair back, mascaraing her near-invisible lashes and eyebrows, and dressing fashionably, she's so beautiful that I can't take my eyes off her. Of course, she's wearing the copycat bead bracelets as well, like half the school.

I was already making more of an effort with my clothes and makeup at school, because of Jase, by the time Plum arrived, but I have to admit that her presence has got me to up my efforts even further. It's quite true that girls dress more for other girls than they do for boys.

So I'm wearing a fitted sweater belted over slim jeans, over boots with a two-inch heel, the maximum height we're allowed. The sweater is perfectly decent, but it does show off my boobs nicely—it's emerald cashmere, with a V-neck— and the belt is ancient leather I got from a secondhand shop, pretty much falling apart, which is the way you signal that you're confident enough not to have to wear designer labels from head to toe. I know I look pretty good, and it helps to take on Plum when I feel reasonably okay about how I'm dressed. Especially now, when I'm reminding her, in code, that she can't mention anything about my previous involvement with violent death.

"Actually, I'd worry more about Lady Wakefield. She's *very* strict about gossip," I say, glaring at Plum. "So I'd watch your step."

Plum rolls her eyes.

"You're *so* lucky that your grandmother runs things around here, Scarlett," she coos mockingly. "How I *wish* I was you."

"Oh, sod off back to the French docks," I say, which gets a laugh from the other girls. Even Susan, who's usually Plum's faithful yet silent sidekick, can't help stifling a snicker.

But as we walk down the corridor in the direction of our respective classrooms, I notice that Taylor's eyebrows are drawn tightly together in a frown of annoyance.

"What's wrong?" I ask. "You weren't wound up by Plum, were you?"

Taylor doesn't answer immediately. In fact, she hesitates visibly, as if she was about to say something and then thought better of it. This is so unlike Taylor that I stop in my tracks, pressing myself back against the wall as the tide of girls rolls past. Taylor stops with me, and as I look at her, she shrugs, an eloquent roll of her powerful shoulders.

"I don't like it when she says I'm butch," she mutters eventually. "She's always doing that."

I stare at her, baffled. If that's the case, why hasn't Taylor stood up for herself? She's never had a problem with doing that before.

"But you *are* butch, Taylor," I say. "You *like* being butch. You nearly punched that girl in the boutique last year when she put some makeup on you."

Taylor looks sullen.

"It's different when *you* say it," she mumbles. "You don't mean . . . "

She trails off.

"What?"

I'm baffled now.

"Never mind," Taylor says quickly.

"Plum's just a total cow, Taylor. You shouldn't pay any attention to the crap she comes out with."

Taylor lets out a huff. "Don't you think that's a little easier said than done? I mean, look at all the hell she's caused you."

There's the oddest expression on Taylor's face, like she's trying desperately to hide something. In fact, it occurs to me, a great deal of Taylor's world is still shrouded in mystery. She rarely talks about her parents, who are archaeologists based on a dig in Turkey. She's got an older brother, who travels a lot, and she barely mentions him either. And if she's ever had a boyfriend, or even had a crush on a boy, she certainly hasn't ever breathed a word of it to me. . . .

Oh.

"What?" Taylor says in her turn. "You look like you swallowed a lemon."

"Nothing," I say quickly.

"Forget I said anything, okay?" Taylor says casually. "See you at one for our run."

I nod and dive into the classroom where I have double Latin, very relieved that Taylor and I don't share any subjects. Because the idea that just hit me is unsettling, and I need some time away from her to process it.

It's true, Plum's always calling Taylor butch, but I always

123

assumed she was referring to Taylor's enviable musculature. I never thought any more about it until now.

Is Plum implying that Taylor's gay? Is that what all those comments really mean—all that needling yesterday about Taylor's being jealous of my kissing Jase, which seemed so ridiculous at the time? Is that what Taylor didn't want to tell me—that she's gay, and Plum's guessed?

And why does the idea make me feel so weird?

Thirteen

I SOUND LIKE LIZZIE LIVERMORE

I've been waiting for Jase to ring me for what seems like for-
ever. My phone's scorching hot from all the times I've picked
it up and called his number, only to hear it click over onto
the answering machine after five rings. I've practically been
stalking him, to be honest. But I can't give up. I need to talk
to him.

I need to make sure he's okay. That *we're* okay.

Because after Plum stalked off and left us alone at the
temple, things were awkward. Jase kept saying it was his fault
that I'd been dragged into all this. No matter how much I
tried to console him, nothing worked.

All that vulnerability, that closeness, that we'd shared
when we curled up together on the bench had evaporated;
we barely even kissed goodbye. I had to grab a library book
and get back to Aunt Gwen's—and Jase had to go and face
the police. The weight of what had happened to his father
lay on us so heavily it was hard to breathe, like it is before a
storm, when the skies are low above you and the air is so

thick with atmospheric disturbance that everything moves more slowly, waiting for the crash of thunder.

And by now, I'm torn between empathy and anger for Jase, because he hasn't even let me know how everything went with the police yesterday. I haven't heard from him since we parted at the temple. Over twenty-four hours. It's not fair of him. I'm so worried, and he must know that! He should at least have sent me a text or something, *anything*, to let me know he was okay. . . .

Finally! The phone's ringing, and Jase's photo has flashed on the screen. I scrabble for the Answer button, so eager that I'm all thumbs. For a moment I'm scared that I've cut him off by mistake.

"Jase?" I say, as breathless as if I just did a five-mile run with Taylor setting the pace.

"Hi," he replies, his voice weary.

"Are you okay? How did things go with the police?"

There's a long pause.

"I don't really want to talk about it," he mutters eventually.

I don't quite believe what I'm hearing.

"You don't want to talk about it?" I say, baffled. "But you have to tell me how it went with the police, at least."

He sighs.

"They took me down to the station and asked me a ton of questions about Dad, what happened that night, did we have a fight . . . made me go over it again and again. I just told 'em I went out for a ride and when I got back he'd gone to bed already. Me and Gran didn't hear him go out, but he wasn't there for breakfast. I mean, we thought it was odd, but we weren't exactly going to start a big manhunt just because he'd gone out before breakfast. And yeah, we'd had a fight, but me and Dad were always getting into it. That wasn't exactly anything new."

His words sound practiced, as if he's simply reciting back to me what he's already told the police. For the first time ever, I don't feel a connection between us, and it panics me.

"So what happens now?" I ask nervously.

"Scarlett." He sighs again. "I'm really tired. I couldn't get much sleep. I've had the police on at me asking questions most of yesterday and again today. I just can't cope with you asking me the same things they did. I'm sorry."

But I'm not asking you the same things, I think desperately. *That doesn't even make sense.*

"Jase, I wasn't interrogating you, I was asking how you are." I know this conversation is going horribly wrong, but I have no idea how to fix it. "I was worried about you."

"I know, I know. I should have rung earlier," he says, sounding even more tired.

It's as if ringing me is an obligation, not what he actually *wants* to do. My panic is increasing.

"I just—" I start feebly, not even knowing what I'm going to say.

But he cuts me off.

"I need to be alone right now," he says flatly. "I'm sorry, Scarlett. I have to go."

"Wait—we can't even *talk*?" I protest.

Ugh, I sound so clingy! Like one of those needy girls boys hate. Oh my *God*, I sound like bloody Lizzie Livermore.

But it's impossible for me to be cool in this situation. Jase

127

is pushing me away at what has to be the lowest point of his entire life. What does this say about our relationship? How can we be boyfriend and girlfriend still if he won't even *talk* to me?

"My head's so messed up," Jase says helplessly. "I don't know what to do or how to handle things. I just feel I'm spinning off somewhere . . . Ugh! Scarlett, look, I've got to go, okay? I'll ring you soon, I promise."

And that's it. The line clicks off. I stare at my phone. His photo vanished when he hung up on me. I can't believe what just happened. Twenty-four hours waiting to hear from him, and all I got was a couple of minutes that made me feel I was being a total nuisance to him.

I realize that I'm actually pacing my bedroom, back and forth, back and forth, like a caged animal, the phone feeling like a lead weight in my palm.

Sod it. I won't let Jase push me away like this. I hurl the phone onto the bed and run downstairs, grabbing my leather jacket and dashing out of the cottage. Aunt Gwen isn't back yet, so I lock the door and head out down the drive in the direction of the Barneses' cottage. I'm worried and frustrated, but at this moment my primary emotion is anger with Jase for stranding me emotionally like this. If I manage to somehow winkle him out of his house, I'll be more likely to yell at him than anything else.

The last thing we need is to get into a fight, I think. *Maybe I should turn around before it's too late.*

But there's no point telling myself anything. Nothing could make me turn back now.

As I emerge from the passageway by the side of the

kitchen wing, I can't see anything in the parking lot but an old blue van, pulled up in front of the cottage and blocking everything else from view. The closer I get, the more that I see it's old, dirty, and dented from years of banging down country lanes.

And then I hear a voice I know too well already.

"You're not welcome here!" it screeches, and something is pounded against the wooden step of the cottage, something that sounds like the rubber bottom of a cane. "You haven't been welcome here since you walked out all those years ago, Dawn Merriweather!"

Ah, the dulcet tones of Jase's grandmother. I'm perversely happy, for a moment, to realize that she's as mean to other people as she is to me.

"But I need to see Jase," says a woman's voice pleadingly.

"He's not here!" his grandmother snaps.

I don't walk round the van. I've got absolutely no wish to have nasty old Mrs. Barnes brandishing her cane at me. Instead, I tiptoe up to it and squint gingerly through the dirty window of the driver's side, getting a fairly decent view of the scene unfolding in front of the Barneses' cottage.

Jase's grandmother is standing on the step, looking predictably unfriendly. Facing her is a slender woman in a padded jacket, her legs skinny in tight jeans, her back to me. The woman's hair is black and wiry, done in stubby twists not tidy enough to be called cornrows, tied loosely together at the back of her head in a thick bunch. As she gesticulates, I see her hand is the color of walnuts.

I've guessed her identity already by the time she says plaintively:

129

"But I'm his *mother*, Dorothy. That's got to count for something!"

"Not in my book!" his grandmother retorts.

"And I know he's here! His bike's parked right out in front."

"He's gone for a walk," his grandmother says triumphantly, and steps back, reaching for the door.

A split second later, Jase looms into view behind his grandmother, his wide shoulders and curly head clearly visible even through the grime on both van windows.

My pulse spikes at the sight of him, a bright white surge of excitement in my veins, even though I'm nervous about his reaction when he sees I've ignored what he said about wanting to be alone.

"Mum?" He sounds genuinely surprised, as if his mother's the last person he might expect to show up on his doorstep. "I didn't know you were here!"

"I tried ringing you, Jase, but you didn't pick up," says his mother plaintively. "It's all around the village, what's happened."

"Those nosy parkers in Wakefield! They've got nothing better to do than flap their tongues over other people's business," interrupts old Mrs. Barnes angrily. "And you, Dawn Merriweather, don't think you're coming inside. This was my home before Kevin brought you back to it, and I never wanted you here, as you well know."

"Gran, there's no need for all this," Jase says wearily. "Change the record, will you?"

He places his hands on his grandmother's shoulders and moves her aside enough so that he can get past.

"I'm off out to have a cup of tea with Mum," he tells his grandmother. "Don't go throwing a wobbly, now, Gran. We've got enough on our plates as it is."

His grandmother gives him a hard look, and I think she's going to launch into a further tirade. But then she clamps her lips together in a tight hard line, turns, and walks inside, slamming the door behind her.

"We can sit down in the staff room," Jase says to his mother.

She reaches up to hug him—not easy, as she's even shorter than I am. Jase, I notice, allows the hug, but doesn't really return it. He pats her shoulder with one hand, awkwardly, his body stiff and resistant.

They turn toward me, and I get my first look at Jase's mother, face-on. Her skinniness and slightness make her look young, but her face belies that. There are lines fanning out beside her eyes, deep grooves worn down from her nose to the outer corners of her lips, gray roots to the thick black hair pulled back from her face. She looks very tired, as if she hasn't had a good night's sleep in years.

But although her eyes are weary, their color is unmistakable. They're just like Jase's: pale amber, clear and glowing golden in the winter sunlight. And her lips are like his too, full and purplish, like a plum with the bloom still on it.

I hesitate for a moment as they disappear behind the van. There's a split second when they're out of my sight, and I could take the opportunity to run away, duck behind the van until they've gone, postpone talking to Jase until he's on his own. Even without my concerns about how Jase will react when he sees I'm here, I'm not sure I want to meet his mother. The rest of his family haven't exactly been my biggest fans to date.

But I must want to see Jase more than I want to avoid being yelled at by yet another relative of his, because my feet refuse to move. And the next moment Jase and his mother emerge from round the side of the van.

I'm not even looking at her. Jase is all I can see. And I don't even stop to register his reaction to the sight of me.

I just run toward him and practically jump into his arms.

fourteen
MUCH TOO MUCH INFORMATION

"What are you doing here?" Jase looks down at me as I step back almost immediately, embarrassed that I overreacted and threw myself at him like that.

Not a good start. But at least he put his arms around me briefly, which is more than he did for his mother.

Don't be clingy, I tell myself firmly. *You are not Lizzie Livermore.*

"You sounded awful on the phone," I explain. "I just wanted to see you and make sure you were okay."

He shrugs. "Well, I'm not okay."

God, everything I say to Jase today is coming out wrong.

"Jase," says his mother eagerly, "is this your girlfriend?"

I hold my breath, waiting. After what feels like an eternity, Jase says:

"Yeah, Mum. This is—"

"I'm so happy to meet you!" she says fervently, smiling at me. "And you're so pretty!" She frowns. "I must have seen you round Wakefield village, you look very familiar. Will you come and have a cup of tea with us? She'll come and have a tea, won't she, Jase?"

I dart a glance over at Jase. I'm feeling more confident now that he's acknowledged me to his mother as his girl-friend, but his demeanor is barely more welcoming than his grandmother's was to his mum. His arms are folded and his shoulders are set, his eyes the darkest amber I've ever seen them.

"Okay, I suppose," he mumbles.

If his mother weren't being so nice to me, I would turn and leave. But I'm curious about her. Maybe this will help me get more of an understanding on why the Barnes and Wakefields have such a dodgy history.

"Then I'd love to," I say, smiling brightly.

. . .

"You know I didn't want to leave you, Jason," his mother is saying plaintively.

"I *know*, Mum," Jase rolls his eyes. "You say this every time I see you."

"Your dad said he'd do all sorts if I—well, better not re-peat that, he was your dad, after all. But he promised me he'd never lay a hand on you." She clutched tighter onto his arm. "He didn't, did he?"

From what Jase has already told me about Mr. Barnes, I know his father didn't keep his promise. Jase looks straight ahead, his voice a dull monotone, as he answers:

"No, Mum, he didn't."

I can't believe his mother doesn't see that he's lying.

But then I think: *She doesn't want to see it. She left Jase with her ex-husband, knowing what he was like. She doesn't want to admit what she did.*

"Have some more tea, Mum." Jase jumps up and takes the disposable cup from her. He glances at me, one of the few times this afternoon he's actually met my eyes. "Want some more?"

"Please," I say, sensing that he needs to keep as busy as possible.

Jase takes my cup as well and crosses the room to the big teakettle. I definitely don't want any more; it's stewed, as thick as pea soup. I could almost stand a spoon in it. Heroically, though, I swig down the fresh cupful he brings back, feeling it burn down my esophagus and settle in my stomach, where it'll probably eat through the lining.

We're in the kitchen staff room, which is mercifully empty, as everyone's busy getting dinner ready. Perched on faded old armchairs whose stuffing is coming out at the seams, we're drinking the lees of the tea that was probably made for the cooks and kitchen staff at six that morning, before the breakfast service. It certainly tastes like it's been sitting around all day.

"Digestive?" Jase says, holding up a battered old biscuit tin.

"Don't mind if I do." His mother takes a few and props them on the arm of her chair.

"She eats like a horse," Jase says to me, with a curve of his lips that's a faint, sad shadow of the easy smile of his that I'm used to. "I don't know where she puts it all."

Staring at Dawn—I can't think of her as Mrs. Barnes

135

somehow—I realize that she's eaten her first digestive biscuit in two swift bites, like an animal given a treat, quick to consume it before another predator can take it away. That's not a bad comparison. There's something wild about her, something furtive, as if she were on the verge of running back into the forest she came from, to hide in her den.

She meets my eyes, and in hers I see fear. Unmistakable, pure, naked fear.

What does she have to be afraid of? I wonder.

"When's your dad being laid to rest, Jase?" she asks.

Jase looks grim. "We can't have a funeral yet. Not till the inquest."

Dawn's hands clutch at her cup in a spasm, her thin fingers sinking into the squashy white foam. "There's going to be an *inquest?*"

"They told me they're not sure it was an accident," Jase says flatly.

My throat nearly closes up. After Dan's death, I know all too well what an inquest is. I had to testify at his. It's like a mini-trial, with a kind of judge called a coroner presiding, and a jury. The coroner holds an inquest when someone dies under suspicious circumstances, or when he wants to confirm that what seemed like an accident really was one. The jury gives a verdict—accidental death, misadventure, suicide, or murder—and the police tend to follow what they say.

It's horribly stressful to be a part of an inquest. Especially when the fact that one's being held means that the police and the coroner have doubts that Mr. Barnes's death was the drunken fall it appeared to be at first. If the verdict doesn't come back as accidental death—God, Jase must be coming apart at the seams just thinking about it.

"Of *course* it was an accident," Dawn says frantically. "He was drunk, wasn't he? He fell down and whacked his head. The only surprise is it didn't happen years ago."

She turns to me.

"You mustn't think too bad of me," she says unexpectedly. "You mustn't think Jase's got a mum who just ran away and left him."

I'm totally embarrassed that she's talking to me about such personal, family stuff. It isn't my business what she did when Jase was little. I flash back quickly to the only mothers I've been around for any length of time, the mums of my ex-friends Alison and Luce. They didn't talk like this. They'd ask us what we wanted for dinner, or say it was time to turn off the TV and do some homework, or tell us off for not carrying our plates to the dishwasher when we'd finished eating.

Normal stuff. Being brought up by your aristocratic, distant grandmother and your loathsome aunt in the grounds of a girls' boarding school doesn't give you a very good perspective on what normal is, but I do know how to recognize it. Normal's easy. It feels simple and right and nice.

It doesn't make you want to writhe around in your chair, let alone clap your hands over your ears and sing *La la la* very loudly to drown out what someone else is saying.

"He was all right before." She leans forward earnestly, fixing me with those hypnotic golden eyes. "Jason's dad, I mean. Oh, he always had a temper, but it never got out of control.

137

Same with the drinking. He wasn't like that when we got married."

This is much too much information! I look frantically over at Jase, but he gives me a look that says, as plainly as if he'd said it out loud, *You wanted to come along, and well, here you are.*

Then he stands up and escapes on the pretense of getting himself some more tea. *Bastard,* I think. *How am I supposed to deal with this on my own?*

Dawn sighs. "All the girls in Wakefield were after Kevin. I couldn't believe it when he asked me out. Our parents weren't keen on us getting together. Things were different then. He was a white boy and my parents didn't like that, and nor did his mum." She pulls a face. "No one thinks twice about it now, do they? But my parents wanted me to marry a nice Jamaican boy with a family like theirs. And his mum was a right old racist, to be honest with you. She didn't have a good word to say to me. But we were so in love. You should see the photos. Kev looked so handsome. And I wasn't bad myself in those days."

She catches the involuntary expression of disbelief on my face, and the lines on her forehead deepen.

"I haven't been the same since I had to leave Jason," she says. "And it was the drink ruined Kev. The curse of the Barnes family. Once they start, they can't stop. His dad drank himself to death too. But don't you worry. Jason doesn't have it. I know the signs, I'd see 'em by now. He takes after our side of the family, and we've got no alkies there, thank the Lord."

Now I'm paralyzed in my chair, unable to move, as if Dawn has hypnotized me with those big golden eyes, like Kaa the snake in *The Jungle Book*. And just as if I were in a trance, she doesn't seem to expect any response from me: she just keeps on talking.

I manage to flick my eyes sideways, urgently looking for Jase. He is standing with his back to the wall, his expression as dark and brooding as if he were Heathcliff on the moors. He looks so tortured. Despite my anger at his refusing to talk to me, at his abandoning me here with his mother, my heart aches for what he's going through.

Dawn takes another biscuit and disposes of it in two swift feral bites. It barely interferes with the flow of her speech. "At first, we were fine. Right up until Jase was five. We settled into the cottage—his mum was off living with her sister in Wakefield village—and it was all cozy and nice. I can't say he was always sweetness and light, but he never drank after dinner and he never laid a hand on me, not really. Not so you'd count it. His dad was long dead and his mum was always hovering round, trying to run our lives, but he told her to sod off, and we were happy, just the three of us. And then, everything changed."

She shivers.

"Like day to night. Just a few days after Jason's fifth birthday. We had a party for him, balloons and cake and everything. We didn't have much money, but we wanted it all nice for our boy. I can still see his little face now—he was over the moon, he was that excited. But just a few days later, Kev came home in the middle of the day with a face like thunder, and went straight for the whisky bottle. And after that nothing was the same."

She wraps her arms around herself.

"I told him I wouldn't stand for it," she says quietly, "and he said I could go whenever I wanted but I had to leave Jason. He'd get his mum in to look after the boy. I couldn't take him with me."

She looks at me pathetically.

"I couldn't stay," she says, her voice rising. "It got so bad so fast that I ran out of there with only the clothes on my back one night, a bare two months after he started necking down that whisky like there was no tomorrow. Didn't even stop to grab one thing I owned, I was that scared. I drove back to my mum and dad's. They tried to tell me I should get Jason back, go through the courts, but Kev came round and said he'd kill me if I tried, and we believed him."

There are tears in her eyes now. But, thank God, Jase is coming back to where we're sitting, concerned at the high pitch of his mother's voice.

"Mum, what are you going on about?" he says, looking deeply embarrassed. "Scarlett doesn't want to know all that old family history stuff!"

Dawn freezes in her seat, every muscle in her thin body seeming to contract. The only thing that moves is her eyes, wild, as she stares from Jase to me.

"Mum?" Jase says, sounding worried now.

"*What* did you call her?" Dawn said, looking at me incredulously.

"Scarlett. Scarlett Wakefield. Did I not tell you her name before?"

Dawn drops her foam cup of tea. It splashes everywhere, a stream of thick dark liquid staining her jeans, splattering onto the floor. She jumps up, patting at herself, and I do too, touching the leg of her jeans, backing away when I realize with great relief that the tea wasn't hot enough to scald her.

I run to the tea table to grab some green paper towels to mop her up with. But as I turn around, I see that Dawn's already moving. Ignoring the soaked front of her jeans, she's heading determinedly toward the door.

"I need to get going, Jason. I'm late for work as it is," she says hastily as I push through the door in their wake.

Outside, she fumbles for her keys, ducking her head as she drags them out of her pocket, refusing to meet Jase's eyes, let alone mine.

"I'll ring you later, Jason," Dawn mutters, swinging open the van door, climbing up into the driver's seat, looking very small behind the wheel of the big vehicle. I notice that she's put an old cushion on the driver's side to sit on, to give her an extra bit of height. The steering wheel's being held together with duct tape, and there are some tools and a rusty old bit of pipe rattling around on the floor. The upholstery's so faded and patched up with more duct tape that you can't tell what color it was originally. Jase's mum isn't exactly living the good life.

Dawn doesn't say goodbye to either of us. She just leans over and grabs the open van door and slams it shut as the engine comes to life, turning over with a noise so rattling that even I, who know nothing about cars, can't help thinking that it sounds like it needs a good going-over by a mechanic.

Jase jumps back as the van accelerates away, the exhaust pipe bouncing and grumbling with a series of grunts, the entire undercarriage sounding ominously like it's about to fall off at any minute.

We stand there, watching the dirty blue rear of the van disappear down the service road, not knowing what to say, not even looking at each other.

Because there's no question that Dawn's violent reaction was provoked by hearing my name. My full name. Yes, she was nice to me, but only before she realized that I was a Wakefield.

I sneak a glance over at Jase. I can't believe what's happening to us. What good is it that he told his mother I was his girlfriend, if he can't even look at me now? He's staring straight ahead. It's as though there's a black cloud hanging over his head. I can almost see it.

I wait for him to speak. I'm wondering what he'll say about his mother's weird behavior. But when he does finally say something, it isn't about Dawn at all.

"I'm going back home," he says, still looking off into the distance. "You've got to listen if I say I need some space. I've got so much going on in my head. I can't deal with one more thing, okay? Not *one more thing*."

He turns to look at me, and there's so much pain and darkness in his eyes. I hate seeing him in so much agony when there's nothing I can do about it.

"I'll ring you when I can," he continues. "But I've got to be by myself right now."

I start to say something, but then I stop myself. No use talking when he's made it clear that's exactly what he *doesn't* want.

I thought I was the person Jase turned to when he had a problem. Him and me against the world. And maybe I am, still, though the way he's looking at me right now, I doubt it.

But what if *I'm* the problem? What if his mum's bolting like a startled horse just now was the last straw for him?

Jase turns and strides away. I stare after him, wondering if this is the last time I'll ever see him as my boyfriend.

I'm so hurt and confused I feel bruised to the bone with it.

fifteen
CRABS AND RAMS

It's still only five in the afternoon, and there's no way I can just go back to Aunt Gwen's as if all this drama with Jase weren't happening. I'm standing here, in the very spot where Jase left me, contemplating my options, thoughts too big for my head swirling round inside it and threatening to make it explode, when I hear someone say:

"What's up?"

I turn around and see Taylor standing in the carriage arch, her head slightly cocked to one side inquisitively. I've been so embroiled in Barnes family drama that I've been neglecting her, and she's been really cool about it. However, I can't help but feel a little uneasy around Taylor right now. I'd hate to think that I have a closet homophobe lurking inside of me, but for the life of me, I can't pin this uncomfortable feeling to anything else.

God, Scarlett, why don't you just ask her? a voice in my head prods me.

I should. I know I should. And I would do it, too, if I didn't have so much on my plate already.

"You look like you're away with the fairies, to use one of your Aunt Gwen's weirder expressions," she says amiably. "Wanna talk?"

This is all Taylor has to say to completely disarm me. The awkwardness I felt a minute ago suddenly vanishes. In fact, I'm so glad to see her I have to suppress an impulse to run toward her and give her an enormous hug.

"Oh God, I *so do!*" I exclaim fervently.

Quickly, I fill her in on what's happening with Jase—his mum's weird reaction to finding out who I am, Jase telling me he needs to be alone. Then, of course, comes the worst part of all.

"And Jase said police don't think it was an accident and there's going to be an inquest," I babble. "I think it's more than he can cope with, honestly."

Taylor furrows her brow. "Huh. I wonder what evidence they found at the scene that would make them think that."

Last year, Taylor and I saw someone die in front of us, blasted by a shotgun. And then we lied to practically everyone about exactly how it happened. We covered up an attempted murder.

Which, horrible though it was, does mean that we find it a lot easier than most teenagers would to speculate about the death of my boyfriend's father without having girlie conniptions.

"I have no idea," I say. "Jase told me that he and his grandmother went up to bed the night before, and the next morning his father wasn't there for breakfast, so they thought he'd gone out early. Jase says his dad must have staggered outside at some stage and gone to the lake, though he can't think why."

"And fallen over and hit himself," Taylor adds. "But the marks we saw on him didn't look like they were made by anything he'd fallen on."

"I suppose he could have walked into a branch," I say doubtfully.

"He'd have had to have run into it at full speed to make that kind of welt on his face," Taylor points out.

"Someone could have hit him across the face with a branch they'd broken off," I suggest.

"Well, yeah—but who'd *do* something like that?" Taylor asks automatically.

I backpedal at the speed of light.

"No, I'm wrong," I say quickly. "Mr. Barnes must have been drunk and tripped and fallen into a tree or something and whacked himself on a branch and . . ."

Taylor's expression is so pitying that it makes my toes curl. And she doesn't say anything, just lets me trail off, which makes it even worse.

"It might have been self-defense," she says eventually.

My head is throbbing all of a sudden. I can't let any of this sink in.

"I know you don't want it to have been Jase, Scarlett," Taylor says, as gently as she can. "But logically, he's the most likely person for the police to look at. They'd had a big fight—threats were made . . ."

I can't meet her gaze anymore. I drop mine to the cement beneath my feet. We've been strolling aimlessly around the back of the kitchen block, past the staff car park, too caught up in solving this mystery to notice where we're going.

"That's not to say it *was* Jase," Taylor adds. "Maybe it was someone with a grudge against his dad, who got him to leave the house somehow."

Adrenaline shoots up my spine. *That has to be it.*

"He *was* the kind of person a lot of people would have a grudge against." I feel a slight release of the pressure clamping at my temples. "Remember I said Jase's mum told me about Mr. Barnes starting to drink so suddenly? It sounds like something happened out of the blue, something really big and bad that changed everything."

Taylor's interest is definitely piqued. "Really? Like what?"

"I don't know," I sigh. "Dawn left before she could tell me why."

Taylor cracks her knuckles, thinking hard.

"You said Jase's mom told you his dad started drinking a few days after Jase's birthday. Which is . . . ?"

"July twenty-fifth," I say automatically.

Taylor breaks into a smug smirk.

"They have all the back editions of local papers in the public library. We can go check out if anything happened around those dates."

Why didn't I think of that?

"Wait, this is sort of like going behind Jase's back," I say, worried. "I don't know how he'd feel about it."

"All of this happened ages ago. He was just a little kid. It's not like you're snooping on him *now*, is it? Besides, Jase is probably too dazed to realize that the police are going to come after him. Don't you want to find out the truth before the cops start harassing your boyfriend?"

I know that Taylor has a bias here: she'll jump at anything that involves an investigation. But she does have a very good point. If we can get to the bottom of all this before the authorities do, it could spare Jase, and me, a lot of heartache.

"How do you know that the library has the back editions?" I ask.

"They always do in detective books," Taylor says firmly. "They used to be on something called microfiche, but now it's all on computers."

Her eyes are gleaming with investigative zeal.

"Race you to the bike sheds," she yells, and takes off.

I'm right behind her. One thing about Taylor: she always provides a brilliant distraction.

* * *

"Tick tock, tick tock," Taylor mutters under her breath, twisting her wrist to look at her watch. "We've only got twenty minutes now before the dinner bell. Half an hour if we bike like maniacs."

"I haven't even got to the right *year* yet," I complain, frustrated. "This terminal's so *slow!*"

"Public libraries, what d'you expect," Taylor says cynically. "At least it doesn't smell of pee since that bag lady wandered off."

"She really did smell of pee." I shudder.

"They ought to have compulsory showers at the entrances to libraries," Taylor suggests.

"Not the worst idea in the world."

I watch the screen slowly, painfully load itself up with a new set of dates. As Taylor predicted, the local paper, the *Wakefield Gazette* ("incorporating Havisham, Ponders Hill, and Milching") has indeed had all its back issues scanned onto the Wakefield Council Web site. The young spotty librarian we asked was very keen to help us access them.

"No one ever asks to see back issues," he said wistfully, "and it was *so* much work to convert them to scannable jpegs. It's nice to see you taking an interest."

Taylor, of course, effortlessly spun a cover story about a school project, but honestly, we didn't even need it. He was just happy to have a task. After he'd helped us, and moved on the bag lady, all he'd been doing was sitting behind his desk, reading a brick-thick fantasy novel called *Dagger of the Elves* and staring surreptitiously at Taylor over the top of it when he thought she wasn't looking.

"Nineteen ninety-six. Got it!" Taylor says happily. "Now, if it doesn't take me an hour to get to the end of July . . ."

Since Jase is two years older than me, that puts his year of birth at 1991. And, incidentally, makes him a Cancer.

Taylor glances over at me.

"I just realized we might be slowing things down by both being on the council Web site," she points out. "Why don't you get off it and let me do this, since mine's going faster?"

I yield to an awful temptation and immediately type the words *astrological sign compatible* into the search engine window. Shortly thereafter, I learn that Jase, as a Cancer, is a sensitive, sympathetic homebody water sign, whereas I, an Aries, am a Mars-ruled fire sign. Apparently, our road "will be a testing one." I also have "unflagging energies and an onward-and-upward imperative," while Jase is "happiest at home" and is "deeply protective of the personal realm," which means that "clashes are inevitable." Above the summary of our relationship, a crudely drawn ram and crab butt heads.

Oh, *rats*.

Of course, I know this stuff is all nonsense: I once heard Aunt Gwen dismiss astrology by asking witheringly what the movement of the planets had to do with her neurological connections, and much as I dislike her, I had to admit she seemed to have a point. So there's no reason that I should be all wound up by the results, especially as the whole part about the "lure of the bedroom" being "strong" is true enough (blush).

Still, it's a bit disconcerting. Naively, I was hoping for a full-on, hundred percent endorsement of Jase and me as a couple, and all these caveats can't help but be worrying.

I'm so distracted by all this that I barely notice when the tapping sound of Taylor hitting the Page Down button stops, because she's found what we're looking for. I only gradually realize its absence, and that's mainly because I'm aware that she's cleared her throat and is still staring at the screen, as if she's trying to call my attention.

I swivel my chair around toward her terminal, drawings of crabs and rams no longer dancing before my eyes.

"Uh, Scarlett . . ." It's very rare that Taylor sounds

hesitant. She clears her throat again. "You might get a bit upset by this. . . . I dunno how to warn you, but did you ever make any connection to the dates? End of July, nineteen ninety-six? Does it ring any, um, personal bells for you at all?"

I look at the screen myself, and all silly thoughts of astrology fade as fast as if someone's wiped my brain settings, because the headline is hitting me like a punch in the face.

Heir to Wakefield Hall Dies in Road Accident!

it's blaring.

Sir Patrick Dead, Wife in Coma!

Taylor reaches out under the desk surface to take my hand, and I let her, though it lies limp in hers because I have no physical sensations at all right now. I'm nailed to my chair and all I can do is stare ahead of me at the copy of the front-page article, dated 1 August 1996, which reads:

> In a terrible tragedy that strikes at the very heart of Wakefield, Sir Patrick, the heir to Wakefield Hall, was knocked off his Vespa motor scooter yesterday afternoon while out for a ride with his wife, Sally, Lady Wakefield. He was killed instantly. His wife lies in a coma at Havisham General Hospital. She is not expected to recover. There were no immediate witnesses to the accident, but farmers plowing a nearby field report seeing a silver or gray van speeding away from the scene down Ditchling Lane.

Sir Patrick and Lady Wakefield are survived by their young daughter, Scarlett, who at four years old is now likely to be tragically orphaned. Honoria, the Dowager Lady Wakefield, declined to comment to our reporter yesterday evening.

That isn't even the worst part. The worst part is the fact that the article's illustrated with a big photograph of my parents on their wedding day, coming out of Wakefield Church, a line of soldiers from my father's regiment holding their swords together to make a canopy as some bridesmaids throw flower petals and my mother's long white veil is tossed in the air by a breeze. It's a black-and-white photo, of course, from a newspaper twelve years old, but it's pretty good quality: their radiant expressions as they look into each other's eyes are enough to bring a lump into my throat the size of a pigeon's egg.

My father's wearing his regimental uniform; he didn't resign his commission till after marriage, and he looks ridiculously dashing. My mother, in a white lace dress and a pearl tiara, is reaching one white-gloved hand up to stop her veil from blowing over her face, laughing with happiness. I think they're the handsomest couple I've ever seen. But then, I suppose everyone thinks exactly the same thing when they look at their parents on their wedding day.

"Scarlett, are you okay?" Taylor says quietly.

"Can you go to the next issue, please?" I respond, in a voice I don't even recognize as my own.

Still holding my hand, Taylor clicks away swiftly with the other, bringing up the following week's edition of the

Wakefield Gazette. It's no surprise that my parents' deaths are still front-page news.

Village Mourns Wakefield Heir and Wife

the headline reads.

Joint Funeral on Sunday Saddest Moment for Wakefield Since War, Says Vicar

Local dignitaries and villagers alike gathered this Sunday for the funeral of Sir Patrick Wakefield and his wife, Sally, struck down in the prime of life by a speeding van in Ditchling Lane as they rode out on Sir Patrick's Vespa scooter last week to enjoy the summer sunshine. Neither the driver nor the van that caused the hit-and-run has been identified, though a police spokesman insists authorities are still following up leads.

Sir Patrick, 33, had a distinguished career with the Royal Fusiliers before resigning his commission upon his marriage to devote himself to the running of the Wakefield Hall estate. His wife, Sally, 34, was about to return from full-time motherhood to her job as a translator when their daughter Scarlett, 4, entered kindergarten in the autumn. Both Sir Patrick and Lady Wakefield were well-known and much-loved figures in the Wakefield area, opening up their historic home for summer fetes, sitting on local committees, and in every way amply living up to the excellent tradition that the Wakefields have maintained for centuries as landowners and guardians of their extensive cultural heritage. They will be sorely missed. Honoria, the Dowager Lady Wakefield, has asked that the family be left alone to mourn at this sad time. Sir Patrick is also survived by a sister, Gwendolen, 37 (in main photograph).

This time, the photo illustrating the front page is of my grandmother and Aunt Gwen flanking me on the steps of the same church, coming out after my parents' funeral. They're each bending down to hold one of my hands. I look chubby and bewildered in my black velvet princess coat and patent Mary Janes. My curly hair is rioting everywhere—my grandmother and Aunt Gwen can't have mustered up the strength it took to wrestle me still while they plaited it into submission that day—and there are tearstains on my cheeks. My grandmother's expression is hard as a rock; she's clearly determined to keep a stiff upper lip. My aunt Gwen is looking down at me, her eyes bugging out with disapproval. Story of my life.

There's another picture below it, captioned:

> Sir Patrick and Lady Wakefield opening this summer's fete a fortnight ago, just days after celebrating their fifth wedding anniversary.

My mother is cutting a ribbon and beaming, wearing what looks like a linen sundress, sunlight glinting at her throat, her hair caught up in a ponytail. Behind her stands my dad, with me in his arms, my smile almost as wide as my face.

"I'm really sorry, Scarlett," Taylor murmurs, clicking off the screen.

I'm grateful that she did. I couldn't have torn my eyes from the picture of my mother at the fete. There's something in it that has made my whole body freeze in shock.

"That's what happened just after Jase's birthday party," I say numbly. "That's what made Mr. Barnes start drinking. . . ."

Taylor's up from her seat and crossing the room, speaking quickly with the librarian. I sit there, still not moving, staring at the blank screen, until she returns with a mug full of hot milky tea.

"Lots of sugar," she says, holding the mug out to me. "I wanted something sweet and he made it for you. He said in England it's the best thing for a shock."

She watches me like a hawk, making sure I'm drinking it all down.

"He says you've got the Wakefield face, by the way," Taylor adds dryly.

"We should be getting back." When I stand up, I'm surprised to find that my legs can still hold me.

"Not till I'm sure you're okay," Taylor insists.

"Please. I need to get out of here."

The bright fluorescent lights of the library, the concerned stare of the librarian behind his desk, the computer still sitting there on the desk with its blank gray screen, everything's suddenly pressing in on me. I have to escape into the dark evening, where things aren't so glaring and I can hide a little. Taylor follows hard on my heels, right beside me as I bend down by my bike stand and start unlocking the chain. Outside it's a full-on winter's night, damp and chilly with a black cloudy sky overhead.

"I can't talk for a bit, okay?" I manage to say to Taylor.

Thank God, she understands. She nods and unlocks her own bike. Then she makes sure I've switched on my lights and rides beside me in silence all the way back to school, not saying a word. But I can feel her attentiveness, the way she pedals her bike next to mine so that she can stop me from riding into traffic.

My grandmother would give her a medal if she were there to see. The last thing anyone wants, I imagine, is another Wakefield hit-and-run tragedy.

I'm amazed I can even pedal. That photo of my mother at the summer fete is dancing before my eyes.

Because in it, the sunlight is shining off the necklace she's wearing, the exact same necklace that Jase gave to me. The one that's around my throat right now, tucked in under my wool sweater. I've been hiding it ever since Plum taunted me about its being cheap. I didn't want to hear any further snarky comments, but I couldn't bear to take it off.

I can hardly believe the evidence of my own eyes. Somehow, I've ended up wearing my mother's necklace.

sixteen

FEELING LIKE A ZOMBIE

I can't face going to dinner at school, sitting at table with the rest of the Lower Sixth, with Plum ready to sink her teeth into me once more. I'm sure she's told everyone about my finding Mr. Barnes's body, even though my grandmother warned us not to speak of it.

I tell Aunt Gwen that I'm not feeling well, make myself a sandwich, and take it up to my room.

I close my bedroom door, lock it, and cross to the mirror, pulling aside the neck of my sweater to examine the necklace once again. The shape is distinctive and unmistakeable. The setting of the stone inside the circle, the delicate chain it's hanging on, even the precise place it sits on my collarbone—there's no question in my mind that the necklace Jase gave me a few days ago, the one with the stone whose color exactly matches my eyes, is the same one my mother was wearing at the village fete eleven years ago.

How did Jase's mum end up with my mother's jewelry? I had no idea they even knew each other! And why would my mother have given Dawn a necklace at all, let alone one she liked enough to wear to a big public event like the summer fete?

My head's spinning. I sit down at my desk and try to eat my sandwich, but it's like trying to chew through chalk. My mouth is dry as a bone and I have no appetite, which is almost unprecedented for greedy me.

I know about how my parents died, of course. It isn't a secret. I hadn't quite realized it was a hit-and-run, though. Since I'd never, ever wanted to hear the details of their deaths, I just filed the story away under "accident" and tried not to think about it too much, because it's so painful. And scary. Accidents are totally arbitrary; your parents can be wiped out, just like that, with no warning, one summer's afternoon, leaving you alone and bereft. Accidents illustrate that you have no control over your life, because from one moment to the next it could be taken away from you.

It never occurred to me that my parents' death might not have been an accident. Why would it?

But now the thought's eating away at me. I can't get it out of my head.

Eventually, I stand up. Without formulating any kind of plan, feeling like a zombie, I leave my room again and walk slowly downstairs, to Aunt Gwen's penguin-filled living room.

She's eating dinner off a tray in front of the TV, something microwaved and calorie-counted. Her eyes bulge in surprise as she sees me sit down on an armchair, dislodging some penguins.

"I want to talk about my mum and dad," I say over the commercial playing on TV.

Aunt Gwen spits her mouthful of Lean Cuisine Cod Mornay back into the plastic packaging. The half-masticated bite looks exactly the same as the grayish fish portion still lying beneath it. Coughing, she fumbles forward, grabs her glass of water, and takes a swig of it.

"*Coming up on E! True Hollywood Story: Demi Moore,*" blares the TV. "*How Demi rebounded from a failed marriage and found herself the ultimate boy toy!*"

Glass in one hand, Aunt Gwen frantically reaches for the remote and turns off the TV.

I've never managed to knock Aunt Gwen this much off-balance before. It's a shame, a small detached voice in the back of my brain observes, that I'm not in any fit state to enjoy it.

"What's brought this on?" Aunt Gwen demands, not meeting my eyes.

"Mr. Barnes's death, I suppose."

I'm not considering my words at all before they issue from my mouth. It's as if something or someone else is speaking through me.

"It made me think about my mum and dad," I continue. "Mr. Barnes died in an accident, and so did they."

Aunt Gwen's mouth is open and flapping like a goldfish's. I wait to see if she'll say anything, but she doesn't, so I go on.

"No one ever really talked to me about what happened to them," I say. "I don't remember that much."

"It was a long time ago," Aunt Gwen says finally. "It was very sad for all of us."

"You must really miss my dad," I press her. "I mean, he was your brother, you grew up together."

Her lips purse as if she just tasted something sour.

"We were close," she says abruptly. "Before he met your mother. Then he was very much absorbed with her."

"And did you like her? My mum?" *Keep pushing*, the inner voice is saying. *Keep pushing till you get somewhere*.

"I really didn't know her that well," Aunt Gwen says, staring at the blank TV screen.

"They lived here for five years," I say tersely. "Ever since they got married. I was *born* here. How could you not know her that well?"

There is a long, long pause. And then Aunt Gwen's head turns, so she's looking directly at me for the first time since I sat down in her living room. If I weren't so insulated by a thick shell of numbness, I'd flinch in fear.

It's like that moment in horror films when the demon that has possessed someone's body finally reveals its presence. The eyeballs flood with black; the head spins round; it speaks in a terrible, grating voice.

I've always known how much my aunt dislikes me. But I've never seen her drop her facade so completely and give me the full, chilling, visible evidence that she actually hates my guts.

"All right, I knew your mother," she hisses. "And she was no better than she should be. That's not what you wanted to hear, is it? But it's the truth. She got hold of your father and grabbed herself a title, and once she'd made sure of him, she started to look around her. It wasn't enough to have Patrick. She had to make every man around want her. And your father was completely blind. He couldn't see what was going on right under his nose."

I can't believe what I'm hearing. Part of me wants to get up and bolt for the door so I don't have to listen to one single more poisonous word from her. But that clear cold voice inside my head, which has taken me over, is saying:

She may never let her guard down like this again. Don't move, and don't say a word.

"I felt *sorry* for him," she says malevolently. "He'd walk around smiling, without a care in the world. Sir Patrick, lord of all he surveyed, with his grand plans for the farm, and his lovely wife and daughter. It turned my stomach."

She pushes her dinner tray farther back on the coffee table.

"Oh, you're his, all right," she adds sarcastically. "You don't need to worry. You're the spitting image of them all. She didn't make *that* mistake!"

My eyes widen to the size of saucers. This is so removed from even my wildest speculations about what might have happened in the past that it has the capacity to shock me still further, even on a day so full of horrible revelations.

But I'm definitely my father's daughter. Even the librarian said it. I'm a Wakefield, and not even Aunt Gwen can dispute that, much as I'm sure she'd love to.

"You can't have been that upset when my mother died, then," I say coldly. "If she was such a terrible person."

I'm expecting her to nod frantically with agreement. What does she have to lose at this stage? But instead she goes very still. I've hit a nerve, but I have no idea how or why.

"I was very surprised," she says eventually. "It was so unexpected, an accident happening like that. Tragic."

"Far too many tragic accidents happen at Wakefield, don't they?" I hear myself say even more coldly.

She looks at me now.

"You mean Mr. Barnes," she says, her face blank. "That was an accident waiting to happen. He drank like a fish. Poor Kevin."

For a moment I debate whether to mention what Dawn told me, about Mr. Barnes's only starting to drink after my parents' death. But my attention has been caught and held by her referring to Mr. Barnes by his first name.

"You and Mr. Barnes were friends." I'm trying to sound as though I know this already.

"No!" she retorts at once. "No, we were most definitely *not* friends!"

And weirdly, this has the total ring of truth. I believe her completely.

"We all knew each other growing up," she continues. "Kevin went to the village school, of course, while your father and I were educated privately. Still, children of the same age, in our holidays . . . it was impossible to avoid a certain amount of contact. I wouldn't call it friendship by any means. Your father and he went to the occasional football game together when they were younger. Drinking in the Wakefield Arms. Your father was generally considered to have the common touch."

She sniffs dismissively, but I know the common touch is a good thing. It means you can get on with people of all different social classes.

She looks at me sharply. "That's why I don't want you seeing Jase Barnes. It's all too easy to make friendships in early life that will hold you back as you grow up. Kevin

Barnes was overly familiar with your father. It made things difficult."

But this doesn't sound right. If Aunt Gwen was worried about Mr. Barnes's being too familiar, why did she just call him "poor Kevin"?

"And what about his wife?" I ask, still keeping my tone flat and even. "Was she too familiar with my father as well?"

"*Her*," Aunt Gwen says between her teeth. "That little mouse, creeping around the grounds, scared of her own shadow. I couldn't bear the sight of her!" She snorts. "She didn't last long, did she?"

She looks at me as if expecting some kind of agreement, almost as if the two of us are friends. This is so bizarre that I can't help shifting nervously in my seat. I feel the detached interrogator's expression slip from my face.

And that's it. The spell I've managed to exert over Aunt Gwen, the one that's allowing me to ask her all these questions and expect her to give me answers, is broken. Strange, isn't it? I managed to stay poker-faced through all her insults to my mother and her comments on my parentage. But when she started acting like I was her best mate, that was when I couldn't keep it together any longer.

Aggression from Aunt Gwen was manageable. Intimacy was definitely not.

Well, the intimacy didn't last long. As I recoil, the aggression snaps right back into place, cutting me off before I can show her the necklace as I'd planned.

"Get out of my living room," she barks at me, shoving back the tray, standing up and flapping her hands at me as if she were shooing out a stray animal. "You interrupt my dinner, ask me personal questions . . . I don't know why I even *talked* to you about Kevin and Dawn. You're a thorn in my side, just like your *bloody* mother. Get out!"

I stalk out of there halfway through this tirade, but I can hear her voice, high and hateful, following me upstairs, until I slam my bedroom door shut so hard it rocks on its hinges.

And then I sit on my bed in the dark, shaking from the release of tension, trying to calm my breathing, rocking back and forth like a crazy person in an insane asylum, quivering from head to toe, until finally I kick off my shoes and crawl under the covers, still shaking, and I fall asleep like that, fully dressed.

seventeen

SIDEKICKS OR RIVALS

"Hop!" Miss Carter screeches. "Left leg! *Left,* Lizzie! Your *other* left! God give me *patience!*"

Sharon Persaud and the hockey girls snicker in unison as Lizzie switches legs in panic and nearly falls over in the process.

"And . . . *change!*" Miss Carter blows her whistle. "Right leg now! All the way across the hockey pitch, come on! Build those quads!"

Plum, wobbling along at the end of the line like an awkward flamingo, wails, appalled at the thought of making her legs any bigger. Even I crack a smile at this.

"I'm *sure* I'm getting my period, Miss Carter," she pleads for the third time this PE session.

But Miss Carter, though young, blond, and comparatively pretty, is as tough as old boots and totally unembarrassed about discussions of bodily functions.

"Nonsense," she bellows cheerfully. "You said that last week!"

"I'm *very* irregular," Plum says quickly.

"Best thing for irregular periods—regular exercise!" Miss Carter retorts. "You run your body, it doesn't run you."

"But—"

"Too many excuses!" Miss Carter blows her whistle again as we all hop gracelessly over the white boundary of the hockey field. "Down on your knees and give me ten push-ups, please!"

Plum looks down at the dirty, muddy grass.

"I'll get *filthy*," she wails.

Miss Carter smiles at a huffing Plum, her white teeth flashing in her rather weather-beaten face.

"Then do full push-ups," she suggests. "You won't get your knees dirty that way. And get on with it. Any more delay and I'll make it twenty!"

I saw Plum in operation at St. Tabby's, and I'm sure the teachers' attitudes here are a huge shock to her. St. Tabby's was such a social school that even the teachers were by no means unaware of which girls were the smartest, the coolest, the most connected to important people in the outside world. Plum exploited her advantages mercilessly. I've seen Mam'selle Bouvier, our old French teacher, playfully adjusting the lapels of Plum's jacket, flicking the tie of Plum's silk scarf, giggling away in French with Plum like a girl her own age as Plum talked her way out of not having done her homework. I've seen Plum widen her eyes and prattle on about the priest-holes at her parents' stately home near Bath, in Somerset, instead of answering a question about the Reformation in history class.

And I've seen her use every single excuse in the book to get out of PE class at St. Tabby's. She was fox hunting at the weekend with the Quorn hunt, and her legs are too sore from taking all those jumps on her new mount for her to do anything. She went to a Northern meeting held by the Duke of Argyll at Inverary Castle, and the Scottish reels have made her ankles too weak to play netball today. She's getting her period, and her Harley Street doctor (the same one used by Princess Eugenie, whom she's *intimately* close to) advises total rest when she's in this condition.

Plum is as sharp as a knife, and she realized very soon that the name-dropping that carried her through St. Tabby's went down like a lead balloon at Wakefield Hall. It only took her a few frigid stares and raised eyebrows from the teachers to stop her tossing out references to famous people she knew.

But her abiding weakness is that she still can't believe that she's being forced to do exercise. And she also can't believe that *nothing* will work with Miss Carter but sucking it up (as Taylor would say) and hopping—on the correct leg—when Miss Carter tells you to hop.

A light rain drizzles down as Plum drops sulkily to her knees and starts her feeble attempts at push-ups. For Taylor and Sharon, this would be an opportunity to show off their amazing upper-body strength. For Plum, it's total humiliation. I haven't been this happy in ages.

"Being thin is not what we care about at Wakefield Hall," Miss Carter says. "Is it, girls?"

"No, Miss Carter," we all chorus.

"What *do* we care about?"

"Being strong, Miss Carter!"

"That's right. Being able to do ten *proper* push-ups!"

Miss Carter stalks over to Plum, who is struggling

167

miserably on the muddy ground. She grabs the back of Plum's T-shirt, where her bra strap would be if Plum needed to wear one, and alternately hauls her up and pushes her down, making sure she completes the requisite number of push-ups. When Miss Carter eventually drags Plum up to her feet, Plum wipes her face with a dirty hand, leaving a big stripe of mucky grass across her forehead. Her expression is absolutely furious.

It doesn't help when Lizzie giggles nervously at the blade of grass stuck to Plum's forehead by a clump of mud.

"Sprint back across the field now, all of you!" Miss Carter shouts. "Then get your sticks and we'll do some goal-shooting practice."

Sharon Persaud is at the head of an arrow formation of hockey girls who shoot off, like a pack of dogs after a fox, their target the hockey sticks piled in the grass. Taylor and I follow more slowly. We do enough running as it is, and we don't want to be knocked down in the stampede. To my surprise, Plum is keeping pace, her storklike legs allowing her to take much longer strides than either of us, though she's puffing for breath. And she gasps out at me angrily:

"I nipped out for a smoke by the barns at lunchtime, Scarlett, and I saw your *boyfriend* going into one of the sheds and running a wood chipper. He looked *very* suspicious to me. He couldn't be concealing *evidence* of something, could he?"

Don't let her get to you! I tell myself firmly, since Taylor, who would normally say exactly that, is resolutely silent as she jogs by my side.

"Oh my God!" I exclaim, easily, because I don't get winded by jogging across a hockey pitch. "You saw Jase *doing*

168

his job! Haven't you got anything better than that? I'm actually disappointed in you, Plum."

I lengthen my stride, till I break into a fast run. Taylor speeds up too, and we shoot away from her, reaching the pile of hockey sticks in just a few steps. As I extract my stick, I look back at Plum, who slowed to a walk as soon as she crossed the field boundary line. She's talking to Susan, and even from here I can see that whatever she said was a barb. Susan flinches and ducks her head, visibly wounded.

"She just took it out on Susan," I observe to Taylor. "I can never get over how mean Plum is to her friends."

"Girls like Plum don't have friends," Taylor corrects me, grabbing her own stick. "They have sidekicks or rivals. I saw enough Plums in high school. The sidekicks never know what's coming next, so they're always wary, and the rivals have to be pretty tough to stick it out."

She looks sideways at me and smirks.

"You're definitely a rival. Especially because you keep challenging her."

"So what about you?" I say, meeting her gaze full-on.

Why aren't you challenging her too? I want to say. But I keep quiet because I'm still not sure I can handle going there right now.

"I'm your sidekick," Taylor answers lightly. "What a dumb question."

• • •

It gets dark by six this time of year. And I want the cover of dark for what I'm about to do.

I feel guilty and ashamed in equal measure. Guilty, because I obviously don't trust my boyfriend at all, if I'm willing to listen to the poison about him that Plum Saybourne's all too happy to pour in my ear.

And ashamed, because here I am, sneaking round the corner of the shed where all the gardening equipment is kept, dressed in all black, acting like a fool. I wouldn't put it past her to have made the entire story up just to laugh at my reaction.

The shed is padlocked, of course. I didn't expect anything else. Not only is the equipment expensive, my grandmother's very strict about keeping everything that's out of bounds locked up. But I've taken good note of Jase's trick for accessing the barn. I circle the shed, trying each loose plank, giving each one a good tug to see if it'll come free at all. A board almost next to the wooden door has enough give in it that I can ease it toward me, making a gap large enough so I can wriggle through the space at the bottom and then work my fingers around it to pull it roughly back into place again.

It smells wonderful inside. Warm and rich with sawdust and freshly cut wood. A small pile of logs is stacked in a wheelbarrow standing next to the wall, its wheels heavily clotted with mud. Wakefield Hall uses a lot of wood as fuel; my grandmother has an open fireplace in her living room, and there are woodstoves in various cottages that need to be fed with staves. Naturally, nothing goes to waste. The small pieces produced by the chipper are used for mulching into the soil. They make really good compost, apparently.

It's standard maintenance work for Jase to be sawing

170

wood and feeding it into the chipper. I don't even know what I expect to find here.

I stand up, dusting myself off, and walk over to the chipper, using the tiny torch on my key ring to guide my way. In front of it there's a pile of wood waiting to be fed in: tree limbs and branches, mostly, but scanning around slowly with the miniature bluish light, I see an old wooden chair frame, its cane seat torn and ragged, broken into a couple of pieces already.

The shape of the chair legs—rounded spokes—triggers a memory in my head.

The marks on Mr. Barnes's body. Long welts that could very well have been made by a blow from a broken-off chair leg.

But as I get closer to the chair, I see that it's draped with cobwebs, pushed off to the side, as if it's been there for years. Certainly it wasn't used on Mr. Barnes a couple of nights ago.

There's nothing else in the pile of wood that looks like it could have been the kind of weapon that inflicted those marks on Mr. Barnes. But now, thanks to the chair, I know what I'm looking for. I walk closer to the chipper itself, the gaping mouth where the wood is fed in. Gingerly, I brush away the thick covering of sawdust and focus my tiny torch on the scary metal teeth.

Slivers of wood are caught all along them. Nothing unusual there. I poke around more bravely now, having checked that the switch on the side is definitely turned off. There's something sticking out of the side, in a gap the width of two fingers between the last steel tooth and the rim of the mouth.

I work my thumb and index finger around it as best I can, try-ing to pull it out. This is where I really need more fingernails than I have. Just a few millimeters projecting beyond the tips of my fingers would really help.

But then, if I were the kind of girl who had fingernails, I wouldn't be poking around in a wood chipper at night, would I?

It's no use. I'll never get it out like this. And the more I try, the more curious I am about it, because it looks a little like the chair leg—from this angle, anyway.

I step back and fish around in the wood pile till I find a slab of wood with a loose nail hanging from it. I work the nail free by knocking the wood on the ground to push the nail back through the hole it made. Then, armed with the nail, I approach the chipper once again. Very carefully, I stick the nail into it as low as I can reach, and use the pointed tip for leverage—the danger is that I'll knock the dangling piece of wood down into the belly of the chipper, where I won't be able to reach it. I wriggle it back and forth, working the piece of wood up toward me until, finally, it's projecting enough from the mouth of the chipper so I can close my fingers over the rounded top of it and drag it loose.

It splinters more as it comes out, because I have to wres-tle it out where it's caught on the side of the tooth. So it's pretty damaged, and it would be very hard to say with any certainty what its original use might have been. The closest thing it resembles, to me, is the spoke of a banister. It's a long, narrow piece of pole, and running my fingers down it, I can feel that it was once smooth and polished. Not a fence pole, or even a broom handle. It's been lacquered at some stage, to give it a shiny finish. Definitely something that was meant for inside a house.

I stand there, running the flashlight over it, squinting hard to see anything out of the ordinary. Halfway down one side is a shadow, and I turn the flashlight to get a better look at it. But the shadow's still there. It's a dark stain of some sort, maybe from mold. Who knows how long it's been lying here in the dirt, waiting to be made into wood chips?

I scratch at the stain with my fingernail. It flakes off. Not mold. My heart jumps into my mouth at the realization of what it could be.

And then I nearly jump out of my skin when I hear an unmistakable sound from just outside the shed.

Someone's sliding a key into the padlock that secures the door.

eighteen

IT COULD BE ALL SORTS OF THINGS

Even I didn't know I could move so fast. Thank God, the wood chips beneath my feet muffle any sound I might make as I dive to the far end of the shed and look around frantically for any kind of shelter in the pitch-dark. I don't spot any, so I curl into as tiny a ball as I can, dragging the sleeves of my black sweater down to cover my hands, ducking my head into my arms so my white face won't show.

The door's being pushed open. Pale light gleams in the doorway, a little illumination from a faint moon, and the next second it's blotted out again as the person who undid the padlock steps in and stands there. I hear the footsteps stop for a moment as, presumably, their eyes become more adjusted to the dark. And then they start again, just a few steps, crossing to the side wall. (I squint through the join of my arms to see that much.) I hear a clicking sound, and with absolute horror, I realize what it is.

In a split second, the shed is flooded with light.

I'm pressed right into the corner. I can't get any lower than I am now without lying flat. I wait, panic-stricken, for a shout, for footsteps to march over to me, or for the sound of a piece of wood being picked up to use as a weapon.

If I hear that, I'll jump up and run, I tell myself frantically. *I can't just wait for someone to attack me.*

There's absolute silence. Which of course could mean that whoever is in here with me is staring at me, incredulous, working out their next move.

And then the footsteps cross to the chipper. I know that much, because I can hear wood being kicked out of the way as they approach it, which means they're moving through the pile of debris waiting to be fed in. I hear another switch being flicked, and then a busy, buzzing noise as the chipper turns over whatever's left in its belly and spits it out.

I lift my head fractionally, just enough to see that I'm actually in a pool of shadow. The single bulb hanging from the shed roof is casting a circle of light in the center of the room but leaving its corners dim.

As long as I don't call attention to myself by making any noise, I should be okay. . . .

I don't dare to turn my head at all. Instead, I slide my glance along to the edge of my eye sockets, which is by no means a pleasant feeling, but just about allows me to get a glimpse of the person standing by the chipper. I have the oddest feeling that it's going to be Aunt Gwen, though I couldn't have said why.

Oh no. That's a lie. I *want* it to be Aunt Gwen. I want it to be her so badly I'm biting my lip with desperation, every nerve in my body aching to see her.

But I bite my lip still deeper with disappointment as I realize the figure beside the chipper is much too wide and tall

175

to be Aunt Gwen. Of course it's Jase. Who else has the keys to the shed, other than his father?

The chipper clicks off again. I don't think he fed anything into it at all; he just let it run for a minute or so. Then darkness overwhelms the shed again. The thin crack where the door is ajar suddenly becomes the only focal point in the room.

My thighs are aching, my feet are hurting where my toes are bent under me, my arms are sore from being raised and wrapped round my head, but I still don't dare to move a fraction. Now that the wood chipper is turned off, the silence in here is absolute. I'm holding my breath, afraid even to let it out.

I can't believe that I'm crouching in the corner of a shed, hiding from my own boyfriend, scared to *breathe*. I've seen people die and I've prevented a murder, but in my whole life, this is the worst situation I've ever been in. Because I'm spying on the person I love.

Then the silence is broken by a strange, gulping noise. For a second I think Jase is throwing up. Then I realize that he's crying—big, heaving sobs that sound dry and painful. A crash makes me open my eyes and focus on where he must be standing. As my eyes accustom themselves to the darkness, I see that he's sent the wheelbarrow that was leaning against the wall flying, its wheels spinning with the force of his kick. And now he's knocking his head against the wooden wall, twice, three times, in rhythm with his sobs.

Oh God, this is so awful. I can't bear it.

But I have to. I have to hear Jase cry his heart out, and

not only can I not comfort him, I'm terrified he isn't just crying because his father's dead, but for something much
worse. . . .

And I'm terrified he ran the chipper because he was worried he hadn't fully got rid of the incriminating piece of wood
he fed into it earlier, when Plum saw him. The piece of wood
I'm clutching in my hand.

The one with the stain on it that looks a lot like blood.

* * *

After dinner, I sit in my room, turning the piece of wood
over and over in my hands, not knowing what to do.

I don't want to admit that I've got any kind of trust issue
with my boyfriend, let alone that I might seriously be sus-
pecting him of killing his—I can't even say it. But the wood
in the chipper and Jase's breakdown in the shed . . . add those
things together and it looks very bad.

I really can't believe that Jase would do any harm to a fly,
let alone his own father. Yet if I went to Taylor and told her
the whole story—or, worse, to the police, God help me—
they wouldn't see the Jase I trust and love. They'd see someone with a motive, opportunity, and now with potential
evidence against him.

I look down at the piece of wood, lightly touching the
stain with my thumb. It could be all sorts of things. Paint.
Spilt varnish. And yes, blood. There, I said it. But honestly,
the only scenario that I can picture that portrays Jase as the
killer is one where Mr. Barnes came after his son and Jase had

to grab something and defend himself. Even then, I'm sure Jase would have rung the police straightaway to tell them what happened. Why wouldn't he?

A branch knocks against my bedroom window, battered by the wind, and I jump; it sounds like that scary bit at the start of *Wuthering Heights* when the ghost knocks on the window, trying to get in. The weather wasn't that bad when I was walking home. There must be a storm coming. Opening my desk drawer, I hide the piece of wood inside, pushing it right to the back. I close the drawer, no closer to understanding what all this means than when I was sitting in the shed's pitch-darkness after Jase eventually locked up and left, more confused than I have ever been in my life.

Wham! The branch clatters against the window so noisily that I jump to my feet, worried that it's going to shatter the glass at any moment. I throw up the sash and reach out into the dark cold night, feeling for the branch so I can try to bend it or break it.

And then I scream like a banshee, because something has just grabbed hold of my wrist. My whole body goes clammy with terror. Frantically, I try to whip my hand away, but I can't, and I look down in panic, shaking. Even though my eyes are glazed with fear, I see a hand wrapped around my wrist. I look down still farther and exclaim:

"Jase?"

He's holding on to the drainpipe with one hand, his face upturned, staring at me, his eyes wide and vulnerable and pleading.

"I really need to see you, Scarlett," he says breathlessly. "Pull me in, *please*."

But seeing Jase doesn't abate my panic, it pumps it up instead. I've broken out in a cold sweat. Because this isn't the first time a boy has stared up at me desperately, hanging from a drop, needing me to pull him up. Last year, Dan McAndrew's brother Callum was clinging to my wrist, his life depending on mine. The flashback is so powerful and intense that I freeze, slapped hard in the face by déjà vu.

And my wrist goes dangerously limp as all my muscles slacken, sending Jase sliding a foot farther away from me down the wall, as he scrabbles to reestablish his foothold.

"*Scarlett!*" Jase hisses frantically. "I'm slipping! *Help me!*"

nineteen

PLENTY OF DARK SECRETS

The naked fear in Jase's eyes and voice pulls me back to the urgency of the situation in double-quick time. Callum McAndrew's handsome face disappears, and I'm more than relieved. I'll never see Callum again. He's the past, and Jase is the present: here, now, in trouble, slipping down the wall, needing my help.

Which begs the question: how much help should I give him? Just enough to get secure again, so he can climb down the drainpipe?

Or should I pull him into my bedroom? Would that be trusting him too much? The Jase just below me, holding my wrist, looking up at me imploringly, isn't the shadowy, suspicious figure I saw earlier in the woodshed. But I remember that figure. I remember hiding from him, curling up in a ball, not brave enough to stand up and let him know I was there.

"Scarlett, I can't hold on much longer . . . ," he entreats.

In the end, it isn't my head that makes the decision. It's my heart, which tells my other hand to reach down and close around Jase's wrist and my legs to brace themselves against the windowsill. My knees bend and take the strain as I start to haul Jase up and into my room.

I may be the biggest idiot in the world. I don't know the truth of what happened with Jase and his dad. I don't know if it's my loneliness that's telling me to let him in, or my good judgment. I don't know if this is a decision made out of weakness or out of strength.

But as he tumbles over the windowsill and climbs to his feet, I burrow into him as if he were a warm blanket I could pull around myself, and he hugs me back just as tightly.

"I'm sorry I was such a prat before," he says into my hair. "I'm so messed up, but I shouldn't take it out on you." He shudders. "It's horrible at home. Me and Gran aren't talking at all."

"When's the inquest?" I ask.

"Tomorrow." He shudders again, worse this time. "I'm just praying to God they say it was an accident and it'll all be over, we can lay Dad to rest and get on with our lives."

"But, Jase—" I start to say.

There's so much I want to ask him: the words are on the tip of my tongue.

Do you know more than you're telling me about your dad's death? What were you doing in the woodshed this evening?

"Don't, Scarlett," Jase says sadly. "Please, no questions. There's stuff I can't tell you right now. I just can't. Can you not ask me anything else? Can you please have faith in me, for now?"

I know anyone would say I'm an idiot for continuing to trust him, especially given what he has just admitted—he's keeping secrets from me. But when I look up into his golden eyes, I can't see anything there but honesty. Reliability. Trustworthiness.

My head feels like it weighs a hundred pounds. Suddenly, I'm so exhausted I can barely move a muscle.

"I'm *so tired*," I whisper, and I know that by not challenging him, by not insisting that he tell me the truth, I've lost my opportunity to push him for answers, tonight, at least.

I remember Jase at the temple, telling me not to worry about my own secrets, that he had some of his own.

He really must be the right one for me, I think with a flash of black humor. *The only guy who probably wouldn't blink an eye at my past is someone with plenty of skeletons in his own closet.*

"Me too. I'm knackered." He sighs. "I had to do some errands today in Wakefield. I mean, I didn't have to—your gran's told me to take all the time off I need—but I thought I might as well keep busy. We needed some things for the house as well, so I just thought I'd take Dad's truck and get some things done. Every shop I went into, people were whispering behind my back."

"Really? Whispering what?"

I stare into his face, willing it to tell me the truth, wanting to read innocence on every feature.

"All sorts of things," he says bitterly. "'No smoke without fire.' 'Why haven't the police just said it was an accident?' That kind of thing. You know, Dad was a right old drunk— no one would've thought twice about it if he fell over and cracked his head open. Which is why I just don't understand what this inquest is about to begin with. The coppers won't tell me why they're not just calling it an accident and letting it go."

It's those marks on Mr. Barnes, I think. I bet the police would love to get a look at that piece of stained wood I found in the wood chipper.

Jase looks down at me.

"Scarlett?" He hesitates for a moment. "Look, I know I've been a moody bastard to you, and I'm really sorry. You've got nothing to do with all of this."

"It's okay," I say, though I wonder if he's right about that last part. I think I do have a lot to do with this, more than I want to accept.

"Can I sleep here tonight?" he asks. "I don't want to go home."

"Here?"

I glance over at my narrow single bed. We'll never fit on that.

"I'll sleep on the floor," he says quickly. "Just being here, next to you, hearing you breathe—that'd be fantastic. Please?"

"We could pull the mattress off and put it on the floor," I suggest. "Then at least we wouldn't be dangling off the edges."

Jase grins for the first time that night. It's only a faint shadow of his usual glorious grin, white teeth sparkling, golden eyes bright, but seeing him smile unlocks something in me, and I find myself able to flash a smile back at him, even if it's only as fleeting as his own.

"That'd be *wonderful*," he says, his tone heartfelt.

Ten minutes later, we're curled up next to each other on

the mattress. Jase is spooning me, his warm body pressed against my back. He's taken off his jacket and boots and pulled his belt out of his jeans so it doesn't dig into him. I'm in the flannel pajamas I was wearing when he came through the window. And though I normally want to have my bare skin pressed against his as much as possible, tonight I'm happy with things exactly as they are—our bodies fully clothed, the duvet wrapped around us, tucked in tightly. Jase kisses the back of my neck as I close my eyes, in the dark now, but not alone.

"Jase?" I say quietly.

"Mmn?"

He already sounds half asleep. We're both completely shattered by the drama of the last few days, and the comfort of each other's bodies is like a drug, knocking us out.

"I never asked if your mother told you where she got the necklace," I say, touching it with my fingertips, thinking of how overjoyed I was when he gave it to me at the café, and how long ago that seems.

"I found it in my mum's room after she'd left," he mumbles into the back of my neck, his lips soft on my skin. "I never saw her wear it, actually. But I knew it'd look beautiful on you."

He squeezes me.

"When I can afford it, I'll get you earrings to match, eh? Same color, like your eyes. Maybe for your birthday. That's a few months away, isn't it? Give me time to save up."

I realize I'm crying silently, tears pouring down my face, so silently that Jase doesn't even notice. The sweetness of his words gave me permission to let go. I've needed this release since seeing him in the woodshed. I probably should ask him more questions, but instead I turn my face so it's resting on the arm of my pajamas, and let the soft, much-washed flannel absorb my tears.

I'm drifting off to sleep, the pressure on my skull melting away. Jase's steady, even breathing settles into a slower rhythm now, the heaviness of his arm across my waist telling me that he's falling asleep too. The weight of Jase's warm arm is dissolving all my doubts, draining them out of me through my silent tears. Sleep rolls over me like a breaking wave, turning and pulling me under, and I let it take me. I'm pulled under by the breaker, and I'm so exhausted that, mercifully, I don't even dream.

* * *

The inquest on Jase's father started at nine this morning, and I've been on tenterhooks ever since. Jase climbed out of my room at dawn and went home to smarten himself up, put on his only suit. Both he and his grandmother have to testify about his father's last hours. I shiver, remembering my own experience of an inquest. Although there isn't a scary lawyer in a horsehair wig who cross-examines you, the coroner asks you all sorts of questions, and that's intimidating enough, especially as you're sitting up in front of everyone in a witness box, all eyes on you. It'll be even worse for Jase, because he knows almost all the participants. The coroner, the police, the jury: they're all from Wakefield. They all knew his dad.

And so they'll all be wondering why something so obviously accidental as a notorious drunk falling over and cracking open his skull merits anything as formal as an inquest, rather than a straightforward assumption of accidental death.

From my memory of the inquest on Dan, I know that before Jase gets called, there'll at least be testimony from the doctor who did the postmortem on his father's body, and the police officer who was first at the scene. I wish I could have gone, but they didn't need Taylor and me to testify about finding the body, because DS Landon had already told my grandmother that we had no evidence to contribute; we didn't see anything beyond simply stumbling across a corpse.

So I sit in class all morning, utterly unable to concentrate. The teachers might as well be talking Cantonese, for all I take in.

We're just going down to lunch when my phone buzzes with a text from Jase.

Meet me @ mine in 10.

"Tell Miss Newman I've got a headache and gone home to lie down," I say to Taylor, and dash off as fast as I can in the direction of the Barneses' cottage.

Jase isn't there. And I know his grandmother isn't either, as she was at the inquest too. So I perch on the steps, and wait until I hear the roar of his motorbike approaching. He pulls up, jumps off the bike, chucks his helmet and keys onto the seat, and walks over to me.

"What happened?" I say.

I don't know what to think or what to hope. Jase wants his father's death to be declared an accident, that much I know. He asked me to put my faith in him, and I want to. After all, Jase might be keeping things from me, but it's a huge leap from that to being a cold-blooded killer. I absolutely refuse to believe that Jase would do anything premeditated and sinister. In the end, all you have are your instincts, and I trust mine implicitly. I'm as sure as I can be that I'm not dating someone who killed his own dad.

"Honestly, I don't know what happened," he says in a tired voice, sitting down next to me on the steps.

"You don't *know?*"

"They got me up on the stand and asked me all sorts of stuff," he says. "It's like being on trial, sort of. It really did my head in."

I nod sympathetically, remembering my own experience: that was exactly how it felt.

"Afterward I was all wound up," he continues. "I couldn't sit still, so I went out and got on the bike. I meant to just ride around for a bit, sort my head out. But then I kept going and going. . . ." He takes a long breath. "Actually, I just wanted to ride away and never come back."

Jase has been staring straight ahead, and he doesn't look at me even now. But he reaches out and takes my hand, weaving his fingers through mine.

"If it wasn't for you, Scarlett, I wouldn't have come back at all, I swear. I'd just have kept on going. There's nothing for me here but you."

There's such a lump in my throat that I can't speak. We sit there, holding hands. Holding on to each other for dear life.

I hear a car coming up the drive, but we don't stir. It

187

could be anyone. Even when the car slows down to make the tight turn through the stone archway, we still can't see it from here; the whole new wing of the school building is in the way.

"That'll be my gran," Jase says as we hear the car looping around the kitchen wing, coming in our direction. "She got a lift there with a friend of hers from the village."

I stiffen, not wanting to encounter Jase's grandmother again, but before I can get up a police car swings around the side of the building and slows to a halt in front of the cottage.

Detective Sergeant Landon and another officer get out of the car. Their faces are steely masks, showing no emotion at all. DS Landon strides toward us, her mouth set, and instinctively, we both stand up, sensing something bad is coming.

"Jason Barnes, I'm arresting you for the murder of your father," she says.

"*What?*" I exclaim.

I look frantically at Jase, expecting him to protest, to tell them that they're wrong, that he could never have done the awful thing of which they're accusing him. But Jase doesn't say a word. He stands there with his hands shoved in his pockets, silent, frozen, as the other officer walks toward him and nods to the open door of the car, indicating that he should get in.

"You do not have to say anything, but it may harm your defense if you do not mention when questioned anything which you later rely on in court," DS Landon continues. "Anything you do say may be given in evidence."

"What's happening?" I demand of her. "Why are you *arresting* him?"

188

"We have no choice. The coroner's inquest brought in a guilty verdict against him," DS Landon informs me.

"A *guilty verdict?*" I'm gaping.

Landon nods grimly.

"It's not that common, to have a verdict against a specific person at an inquest," she says. "We were expecting a verdict of murder against person or persons unknown. But it's policy to respect the jury's decision in this kind of case, arrest him and take it to trial. I can't say it looked good, Jase's leaving after he gave his testimony. And"—she gives me a very direct look—"evidence came out against him that you may not be aware of, Scarlett."

My heart sinks into my stomach like a cannonball dropping with a thud. I don't even know if I want to find out what's behind her words.

Jase is walking toward the car. They aren't handcuffing him, which is a huge relief; I don't think I could bear to see Jase in handcuffs.

"He'll need a lawyer, won't he?" I ask in a small frightened voice, and DS Landon nods.

"I'll go straight to my grandmother," I call after Jase as he climbs into the backseat. "Don't worry."

Don't worry. Of all the ridiculous things to say.

The police slam the door on him, then get into the car themselves and start the engine. As I watch, still unable to believe what's happening, the police car pulls away, with my boyfriend inside it.

Under arrest for the murder of his father.

Twenty

"YOU SHOULD WALK AWAY"

I tear into my grandmother's office like a maniac. Penny, her secretary, chases me in, apologies pouring from her lips.

"She just ran right in and past me, Lady Wakefield. I couldn't stop her."

My grandmother, sitting behind her desk, raises a hand heavy with rings.

"It's all right, Penny," she says calmly. "No doubt Scarlett has a good reason for this unprecedented interruption. You may leave us."

My grandmother is so unflustered by dramatic situations that she could give lessons on composure to the Queen. As Penny closes the door, I meet my grandmother's clear blue eyes. Her white eyebrows are raised, her hands folded in front of her on the leather blotter resting on her desk.

"Would you care to tell me what crisis is so pressing that you can't even wait to let Penny inform me of your presence?" my grandmother inquires.

"It's Jase Barnes," I say, catching my breath, trying not to appear too out of control. There's nothing Lady Wakefield hates more than a girl who seems out of control. "He's just been arrested for murdering his father. They had the inquest on Mr. Barnes this morning and the jury brought in a guilty verdict against Jase."

My grandmother's eyebrows rise even higher.

"Dear me," she says.

Coming from my grandmother, this is very strong language indeed. With not a word more said to me, she presses a button on her desk phone, which buzzes Penny on the intercom.

"Penny, can you call Jennings immediately?" she requests. "Tell him young Jason Barnes has been arrested and we'll need a good criminal solicitor. I have absolutely no idea how these things work, but hopefully Jennings will."

Jennings is the family solicitor. My heart jumps in relief. I was so hoping my grandmother would help, but I didn't think it would be this easy. When her brief conversation with Penny is finished, she folds her hands again, looking at me, and dips her head in a short nod that indicates I should sit down.

I obey. It's dawning on me that I may have got a lawyer for Jase, but I'm going to pay for it now. If I'm not mistaken, my grandmother is wearing that look that says a lecture is on its way.

I get ready to take my medicine.

"Scarlett," she says eventually, lifting one hand to touch the pearl necklace she always wears. "I want to make one thing clear: I have no interest in asking you intrusive questions about your friendship with Jason Barnes."

Thank God.

191

"Not, at any rate, at this particular moment," she adds. *Oh, damn.*

And I can actually swear that I hear a softening in her usually clipped tones, a gentleness that, coming from anyone else, I would identify as sympathy.

Sympathy from my grandmother? I brace myself against the straight back of my chair. *Oh my God. This is not going to be good at all.*

"I have been observing Jason Barnes as he has grown up, and I have nothing but respect for him," she observes. "He is a good, hardworking boy who seems to be making the best of a difficult family situation. Unfortunately, I could not have said the same for his father, who was a very troubled man."

She sighs.

"Like you, I am extremely reluctant to feel that Jason had any degree of involvement in the tragic death of his father," she says. "But the guilty verdict at the inquest does not bode well, does it? Scarlett, I would advise you to prepare yourself for the worst. If it does turn out that we are both wrong, I'm sure there will be a *considerable* number of extenuating circumstances. And a good solicitor will know how to use those to best advantage."

My eyes widen in horror. She's saying that it's actually possible that Jase might be guilty. But it's as if a steel wall just slid down, separating me from her words. I realize, with a cold, slicing clarity, that the only thing that would make me believe he *is* guilty is if Jase told me so himself. I refuse to accept it from anyone else.

"However, Scarlett, extenuating circumstances or not,"

my grandmother continues, "there is one thing I absolutely must make clear. Should he be convicted, there is simply no possibility of your continuing any kind of relationship with Jason Barnes. You are a Wakefield of Wakefield Hall. I will not tolerate my granddaughter's being involved in any way with a felon."

"But what if Jase didn't do it," I blurt out, "but it looks as if he did? What if he gets convicted even though he's innocent? That happens sometimes. I know it does!"

Lady Wakefield purses her lips.

"Miscarriages of justice do happen, even in England," she concedes, "though I am happy to say that they are extremely rare. But I am afraid that my edict would not alter in any way. If Jason Barnes were to be convicted of his father's murder, I would forbid you to have any further contact with him."

"But—"

"Scarlett," she says very quietly, and all the hairs on the back of my neck stand up. "It would be utterly and completely out of the question. Please believe me when I say I would do everything in my considerable power to keep you and Jason Barnes apart, for your own good. I cannot imagine you would want to put me to the test."

This makes my aunt Gwen's threats to enforce some kind of house arrest for me pale by comparison. Aunt Gwen could scream and shout all day, and it wouldn't be as terrifying as a few softly spoken sentences from Lady Wakefield. I know she means every word. If she has to ship me off to some reform school up a mountain peak in Switzerland run by psychotic nuns, she'll do it. No question.

My mouth's gone dry. I manage a nod of submission.

"I'm glad I have made myself clear," she says, and again, the note of sympathy in her voice is the biggest warning of all.

Because it's the tone you take when you're breaking the worst news possible. When you tell a person that someone they love has just died.

. . .

I told Lady Wakefield that I would go straight back to class. And I lied through my teeth. As soon as I'm clear of her suite of rooms, I'm bounding along the corridors, the length of the building, down the far stairs and outside, around the art block to the Barneses' cottage. My bicycle is parked in the bike sheds, but a bicycle won't get me where I'm going nearly fast enough.

How hard can it be to ride a motorbike, anyway?

The keys and the helmet are still on the seat of Jase's bike. There's a spare pair of gloves for me under the seat, and I grabbed my jacket from the cloakroom on my mad dash through school. I'm as ready as I'll ever be.

I just can't think too much about what I'm doing, or I might lose my nerve completely.

If I weren't used to riding on the bike with Jase, I think I'd probably fly straight off the back as the bike lunges into a tree when I fire it up. It's that powerful. Like you see in the films where people shoot a big gun for the first time, and the recoil knocks them off their feet. I'm bracing myself with every muscle in my body, thighs clamped round it, biceps tensing with anticipation of the thrust.

And even then, even with all the strength I have from years of gymnastics plus daily workouts with Taylor, I can barely control it. The motorbike is built on a huge scale, which is a gigantic problem for me, as I'm much smaller than Jase. It's a real stretch for me to reach the handlebars and stay on the seat. Still, I keep my legs down, feet pressing into the footpegs.

For a moment, I panic, thinking, *I can't do it! I can't hold it!*

And then, as I freak that the bike will get away from me, I find another inch of length in my back, enough to lean forward even farther, right over the handlebars. I push my legs down as hard as I can, lengthening out my back even more, and pretend my old gymnastics coach, Ricky, is pressing on the small of my back with everything he's got. And suddenly, as I fly down the drive, the wind whipping at the front of my body, it all comes together.

It's like riding a tiger. The bike surges beneath me, carrying me along, and I have to be brave enough to master it, because if I lose my nerve, I'll be in the worst trouble I've ever known. I know how Jase turns the bike, because I've learned to lean with him. He says it's called countersteering; you turn away from where you're going, not toward it.

I'm at the bottom of the drive. I need to go left, for Wakefield village, and there's no traffic at all. Even with my torso stretched almost flat over the bike, which makes it much harder to turn my head, the visibility is really good for this turn. It's winter, and the trees are leafless. If there were a car or a bike on the road, I'd see it immediately.

I'm slowing down but I don't need to stop. Nothing to watch out for, and no ice on the road. I can make the turn, I can go for it—

Turn it to the right, I tell myself. *Do what your head says, not your instincts.* As I turn the handlebar to the right, the oddest thing is that it actually feels like I'm pushing the left grip rather than pulling on the right one.

Emboldened, I turn it more confidently, more and more, and the harder I push it, the more the bike turns to the left. My head is spinning with excitement and my whole body is throbbing with the revs of the bike as I turn onto the main road.

I forget to lean. Or I don't lean enough. I don't know what I do wrong, but the bike wobbles and tilts. It's only by the grace of God that I manage to get it straight again. I scream in fear and the scream reverberates inside the helmet, freaking me out still more, the sound of my own voice shrieking because I thought I was going to crash to the ground with hundreds of pounds of motorbike on top of me.

Staycalmstaycalmstaycalm! I babble to myself. *Stayalivestayalivestayalive!*

I ease off on the throttle, having scared myself half to death. *No point getting there in a body bag.*

By the time I reach the village, my heartbeat has slowed down to something that's certainly not normal, but at least allows me to breathe without thinking I'm going to choke every time I inhale. Right now my rib cage is contracting in panicky spasms. I manage to get it under some sort of control,

196

even as my hands slip in my gloves, sweaty with fear. *You're doing fine,* I tell myself firmly, tightening my grip. *Not much farther now.*

I've got to get to Jase. I've got to tell him I'll stand by him.

I can't believe I might have to choose between him and my grandmother.

I can't believe Jase might go to *prison.*

I can't believe what my life has turned into—just when I thought it was actually coming together. . . .

Thank God Wakefield village can't help but have a calming effect. Like Plum and her London set, it's *very* concerned about appearances. The fact that it won Best Hanging Baskets in the Small Village category of the Best of Britain's Gardens competition is announced on blue commemorative plaques everywhere you look, even though on this wet damp day in February the hanging baskets are just boasting some mildewed-looking pansies. Since my grandmother (who owns most of the village) is very keen on tradition and keeping up standards, every building over a hundred years old has been carefully restored. The High Street's often used for filming scenes from period dramas. We've all got pretty used to having its cobbles strewn in hay so carriages can roll down them, carrying girls in bonnets.

What used to be the police station, a nineteenth-century brick building covered in ivy, is now a quaint hotel called (with great originality) the Old Police Station. Tourists love it. The new police station is tucked away behind a roundabout, beyond the petrol station and the supermarket. It's a nasty single-story 1970s building with low ceilings and no architectural merit at all, but that doesn't matter because the tourists never see it. There's hardly any crime in Wakefield village, anyway.

Till now.

You wouldn't even know it was a police station without the blue light hanging over its entrance, and a couple of police cars parked in front. Thank goodness, there are no officers hanging around beside them as I gingerly veer into the parking lot, remembering to lean properly to make the turn. I zoom past the cars, jam the brake on too heavily, and skid to a horrendously awkward halt that ends up with me and the bike mere inches from the back wall of the parking area.

My wrists are killing me. I was leaning forward so far that most of my body weight was on my hands, and of course I was gripping on like a madwoman for dear life. I sit there, the blood still roaring in my ears, and try to calm myself, flexing my hands and wincing at the pain as the blood rushes back into my fingers.

I can't reach down and access the kickstand. I'm too short, or it's too awkwardly placed for me. I have to clamber off, hold the bike in place, and wrench out the stand, amazed that my wobby legs are even holding me up. The shock of what I just did, the sheer craziness of it, is almost unbelievable. I *had* to get to Jase as soon as possible. I *had* to let him know that a lawyer is coming, that he isn't alone.

I'm just really lucky I didn't kill myself and wreck his bike in the process.

I'm boiling up. Unzipping my jacket, I pluck at my T-shirt and sweater as I enter the station, trying to cool off my overheated skin. I hope that my deodorant and body spray are still doing their job at two in the afternoon, hours and hours after I put them on. Inside it's a lot less intimidating than I imagined it would be, probably because the police stations you see on TV are in crime-infested cities, not some quiet village where not much ever happens. It's painted white, there are posters everywhere about community policing and Crime Stoppers, and the reception desk doesn't even have glass in front of it. There's less security than in a bank.

Down the corridor is a waiting area with plastic seats, and a couple of people slumped in them with saggy postures that tell me they've been sitting there for ages. Standing at the reception desk, talking to someone behind it, is DS Landon. The woman who arrested Jase.

For a crime I refuse to believe he committed.

"Um, excuse me?" I say, bravely approaching her.

DS Landon swivels round, her eyebrows rising when she sees who I am.

"Scarlett Wakefield," she comments flatly. "Aren't you supposed to be in school?"

"I came to tell Jase my grandmother's getting a lawyer for him," I say, dodging the question.

"Not a good idea," she interrupts.

"You're joking," I say angrily. "He's been *arrested*. He needs a lawyer."

"No, that's not what I'm saying." Landon shakes her head. "Your being here is not a good idea."

"What?"

She looks at me seriously. "Come with me, Scarlett."

She leads me down the corridor and pushes open an orange-painted door, nodding to me to follow her inside. It's a small interview room with a table and four chairs, two on each side. Landon pulls up a chair and sits down, gesturing to me to take the seat opposite her.

"I can't talk to you officially without your guardian being present," Landon says, pushing back her hair with both hands. It's straight and blond, cut too short to be a bob, but just long enough for it to be hooked behind her ears. She isn't wearing any makeup, and there are faint dark circles under her eyes. She looks pretty stressed.

"And," she continues, "I probably shouldn't be saying this to you at all. But you're Scarlett Wakefield, and your grandmother is who she is, and you're the motive here, okay? That wasn't mentioned at the inquest. But why do you think they found Jase guilty?"

I stare at her blankly. "I don't understand."

"Scarlett, you're Jase's *motive*. That's why he was fighting with his dad. We talked to some girls at your school the afternoon you found Mr. Barnes's body. Someone called Plum in particular. She said you two were a couple, you and Jase. And the more we asked around, the more we found out his dad was really unhappy about it."

"But that doesn't prove anything," I protest. There's no point my denying that Jase and I are together; that would look really suspicious in itself. "I mean, so his dad wasn't that keen on our seeing each other. So what? Parents get cross about who their kids are seeing all the time. Jase wouldn't *kill* him over that!"

"I agree," she says, surprising me. "But, Scarlett, the medical evidence is clear. His dad didn't fall over and hit his head and die by that lake, like Jase wanted us to think. He was carried there after he died. The lividity of the corpse proves it. In fact, it appears that Mr. Barnes was transported there in a wheelbarrow. We found fibers of the jacket and trousers he was wearing inside a wheelbarrow on school property. There's no way they would have got caught on the bottom of the wheelbarrow if he hadn't been physically inside it. Besides, Mr. Barnes had defensive wounds on his arms, which means he was fending someone off. This was no accident."

Oh God. The wheelbarrow tracks on the grass by the lake. I thought they were old, but they must have been made when Mr. Barnes was taken there. And all that mud on the wheels of the barrow inside the woodshed. Not just from the lawn, as I thought. That came from wheeling a heavy load right through the grounds and into the soggy grass of the lake borders.

I can't say a word.

"Scarlett, there's a jury verdict now," Landon points out. "That changes everything. Apparently every single person in Wakefield village is convinced that Jase finally gave his dad what was coming to him. And we're sure that Jase lied to us about not knowing how his father's body got to the lake. Besides, he's refusing to say a word to us now. Not a single word. Why won't he talk, unless he's got something big to hide?"

She gives me a narrow-eyed look.

"The best thing you can do for him now is to tell your boyfriend to come clean and admit what really happened, okay? This wasn't self-defense. The marks on the body prove that, I'm afraid. But if Jase'd come clean and plead manslaughter, we'd accept that."

It was my last hope, that Jase could claim it had been self-defense. I stare at her numbly.

"Scarlett, listen to me," DS Landon says. "Your boyfriend's got a nice clean motive, something a jury will understand right away: young love. Everyone remembers what that felt like. Your aunt wasn't keen on your seeing him either, was she? We've got a witness from a coffee shop in Havisham who told us your aunt dragged you out of there a while ago because you were sitting with Jase Barnes. Everyone was against you, weren't they?"

The sweat has dried on me now. I'm cold as the grave.

"Best thing he can do is fess up," DS Landon says. "Because if this goes to trial, your name'll be dragged into it. No way that can be avoided. Don't tell me Lady Wakefield's going to fork out for expensive lawyers just so her granddaughter's name will be splashed all over the papers. She might even cut the funds off, and then where'd he be? Stuck with a legal-aid lawyer who doesn't know his arse from his underpants."

Oh God. She's right. My grandmother might even do that.

"We won't be hard on him," Landon adds. "You're right. His dad was a drunk, and a nasty one. Knocked his mum about till she left him. Everyone in Wakefield knows Kevin Barnes had a temper. Jase has never been in trouble before, his record is clean. That'll go a long way for him. But he's got to tell us the truth, okay?"

Oh no—Jase and his secrets. They're all going to come out now.

Landon keeps on pushing me. "Who else but Jase would have dumped his dad's body by the lake? Who else would know where to go, and where to find the key to the gate? It was stupid of him to try to pretend it was an accident, but he's only a kid. It's not too late for him to make it all right."

The trouble is, everything she is saying makes sense. I've asked myself those identical questions, and Jase's has been the only name I could come up with.

"You tell him to come clean, Scarlett." Landon stares at me hard. "And then you should walk away. Your gran won't want you mixed up with someone in prison. A girl with your advantages—you can do a lot better for yourself than a boy who's doing time."

God, it's like a broken record! I grit my teeth in anger at all these adults trying to run my life for me.

"Sarge?" A young constable pushes the door open and pokes his head in. "A lawyer's turned up for Jason Barnes. Shall I take her in?"

"I'm on it," Landon says, rising to her feet. "Perfect timing. We're done here."

By the desk is a woman in a dark trouser suit, a briefcase in her hand. She turns as Landon walks toward her, and says:

"Jas Ramu. I'm here to represent Jason Barnes. I understand you have him in custody?"

"That's right. I'm DS Landon, the arresting officer," Landon says, nodding at her. "I'll take you in to see your client."

But they're interrupted by someone sitting in the waiting area, who jumps up on hearing this exchange.

"I'm Jase's mum!" she says frantically to the solicitor. "What's going on? They said Jase was arrested, but no one's told me what's going on. I've been worried out of my mind!"

"Let me talk to my client first, Mrs. Barnes," Ms. Ramu says briskly. She's small, with slicked-back hair, thick and black as a crow's wing, and dark coral lipstick that matches her silk shirt. Her smart appearance is reassuring—she looks as though she could take on the whole jury by herself. "Then I'll have a better idea of what's going on, and I can fill you in."

"But I want to see him," Dawn wails. "I'm so worried!"

Her thin body seems to crumple in on itself. Hugging herself around her waist, she looks pitifully fragile, the bulky parka that she's wearing hanging off her bones as if from a wire hanger. Her face is a mass of creases. She looks very small and frail. No wonder I didn't recognize her before, bundled up in that big jacket, its hood half covering her face.

"We'll have him out on bail before you know it, Mrs. Barnes," says the solicitor, patting her hand.

"Bail?" I say quickly, thinking that though my grandmother might be willing to pay for a lawyer for Jase, she'll be much less keen to have him released from custody so he and I can see each other. "I have a big trust fund. I can put up money for bail if you need it."

Both the sergeant and the solicitor grin at this, identical sardonic smiles.

"American police shows have a lot to answer for," DS Landon sighs, and Jas Ramu says more kindly:

"You must be Scarlett Wakefield, right? We don't do that

whole bail bondsman thing in the UK. Though you're not the first to think so. Bail here just means that the suspect is released before trial, okay? No money involved. It's very straightforward."

She nods at both of us and walks down the corridor after DS Landon.

Dawn and I are left standing there, staring after them, both of us yearning to follow to see Jase. She lifts her head to look at me, and again, it's a visceral shock to see Jase's golden eyes in her small, dark, lined face.

"You seem like a nice girl," she says sadly. "You were friendly, and you listened to me. But then I realized who you were. I should have seen it straightaway. Of all the girls he could have picked. Jase could have his choice of anyone. But a *Wakefield*? As if we haven't all seen where that could lead."

I turn away. Thoughts of what DS Landon just said to me are spinning in my brain, keeping most of Dawn's words from sinking in. In less confusing circumstances, I would produce the pendant her son gave to me and ask her where she got it; right now, I'm too overwhelmed to open that can of worms and heap its contents on top of all the other mess I have to deal with.

Without a word, I walk outside to get some fresh air, and the door bangs behind me. Then it opens again, and Dawn patters out in my wake.

"I didn't mean to upset you," she says. "I'm sorry, I'm all over the place, I don't know what I'm saying. Oh God, I need a fag."

I look around to see her patting the pockets of her parka hopelessly.

"You don't smoke, do you?" she asks.

I shake my head.

"I've got some in the van," she mutters, crossing to the dented old van drawn up wonkily off to the side of the parking lot, taking up two spaces. "I know I shouldn't smoke, okay? Jase is always going on at me. But it calms my nerves. I try to stop, but it never lasts."

She's twice my age, and here she is acting as if I'm the adult and she's the child. It's definitely weird. I find myself walking by her side, almost as if I'm protecting her, but from what I have no idea.

Maybe from herself.

Dawn hasn't even locked the van, but I can't say I blame her. Stealing a vehicle from outside a police station would be idiotic, but anyone who chose this scratched, beaten-up old banger would be clinically insane. When the door swings open, a bit of pipe falls out at our feet, and as I jump to avoid it Dawn says:

"Things just keep dropping off the bottom, it's that old. I pick them up and save them, just in case they're important. But it's still running, so it can't be that bad, can it? Makes a terrible racket, but they all do that after a while, don't they?"

I bend down and pick up the pipe, not knowing what to say. But as I slide it back along the floor of the cab, where it joins the other rust-stained debris knocking around in there, an awful thought strikes me.

Mr. Barnes was hit across the leg with something just like this pipe.

I back slowly away from the van, and as I do, I notice for the first time that, under the flaking navy paint, the van isn't chipped down to the metal as I thought it was before. There are layers of old paint underneath. And the bottom layer looks very pale. I reach out and rub at one of the peeling patches, picking off another bit of the dark blue, uncovering what's underneath.

White. So dirty it's almost colorless. But it's definitely white paint.

My parents' deaths and Mr. Barnes's recent demise flood together in a series of terrifying connections.

Did Dawn drive the van that killed my parents? Is that how she got my mother's necklace? And did she kill her husband, too?

Is that why Jase won't tell the police what really happened last night, why he won't even tell me all his secrets? Is he covering up for his mother?

Frantically, I process my ideas. I can just about see skinny, frail Dawn physically able to hit a drunk Mr. Barnes across the legs with a pipe; if she got up a good swing, the weight of the iron would do enough damage to knock him over. But there's absolutely no way that Dawn's birdlike frame is strong enough to have picked up burly, overweight Mr. Barnes, put him in a wheelbarrow, and dumped him by the lake.

That must have been Jase. I face the fact squarely. DS Landon's right, there's no way around it. Jase must have been the one who dumped his father's body.

And since I refuse to believe that Jase had anything to do with his father's death, he must be protecting someone. It would make total sense if that person were his mother.

But what would Dawn have been doing at the cottage late at night? I remember Mr. Barnes, drunk, abusive, flailing around, as I watched the scene through the window. Dawn would remember all too well what her husband was like when he was drinking. She'd be very unlikely to go near him in the evenings, when he'd be at his worst. It's possible that she had to see him for some reason that wouldn't wait, and took a pipe from her van to protect herself . . . but that sounds so dramatic, like something from an action movie. It doesn't seem to fit with Dawn. She's not exactly a kick-ass heroine out for justice.

Also, she's showing absolutely no reaction to my having handled that bit of pipe. As she meets my eyes, all I see in them is shame, and concern for Jase.

My instinct is telling me that Dawn wasn't involved in her husband's death.

"Did this use to be yours?" I hear myself demanding urgently, wrenching the necklace Jase gave me out from under the neckline of my sweater.

"Where did you get that?" she says, her eyes widening, the cigarette trembling in her hand.

"Jase gave it to me," I say, looking at her closely. "He said he found it in your room but you didn't take it with you when you left. So he thought you didn't want it."

"His father gave it to me, but there was something fishy about the whole thing. He told me not to show it round, to just wear it in private. And he never gave me presents at the best of times. I thought he'd nicked it, to be honest. Stolen goods. I didn't want anything to do with it."

I start to ask her another question, but tears are welling up in her eyes.

"I know I haven't been much of a mother to Jase, but that doesn't mean I don't care. He's everything to me. I gave birth to him, and though I'm sure you won't believe me, I'd give my life for him, I swear!" she wails, wrapping her arms around herself protectively, the half-smoked cigarette falling to the concrete.

I must have been mad to think she could have killed anyone. This pathetic creature couldn't harm a fly. I look at the white paint of the van, then down at my necklace, struggling desperately to put all the pieces together.

And then I take in what she's just said, how much she loves Jase. I hear her sobs, and I believe her completely. There's no deception about Dawn, no cunning plan to take me in. She simply wouldn't be capable of it.

So if I believe her—which I do—she couldn't have killed her husband. Because if Dawn saw Jase arrested for something she'd done, she wouldn't be out here crying hysterically. She'd be marching into the police station to confess and clear his name.

My brain's spinning so fast I actually clamp my hands to my skull, holding it still. I can't cope with a single further thought or speculation right now.

All I know is that Dawn had nothing to do with her husband's death. And I simply can't believe she killed my parents, either.

Then who did?

God, no. No more. I turn away from Dawn and practically sprint toward the motorbike. If I don't clear my head, I honestly think it will explode.

Twenty-one
"LITTLE MISS NOSY"

The bike skids sideways across the parking lot and slides to a halt by the side of the Barnes cottage in a maneuver that would be incredibly impressive if I'd planned it. Actually, I misjudged how much room I'd need to brake, and twisted the handlebars in last-minute panic to avoid crashing into the cottage wall. I still can't get the kickstand down the way Jase does it, with one thrust of his booted foot before he swings himself off the bike, but that must be because I'm not tall enough. When I try it I almost lose my balance and fall off the bike.

I clamber down and take off the helmet, propping it on the seat. I have to dash back to school briefly, which is really annoying, but it can't be helped; there's something I absolutely have to do. It barely takes ten minutes before I'm back at the cottage, walking up the steps, knocking on the front door with a steady rhythm that rattles the glass in the panes and doesn't let up until I see Jase's grandmother hobbling across the hallway. She does a double-take when she spots me, rearing back like a cobra, both hands planted on the top of her cane.

"I told you to stay away from us," she snaps, loud enough for me to hear her through the door.

"Let me in," I say firmly. It's not a request but an order.

Right now I feel strong enough to kick the door down if she doesn't open it. And she can hear it in my voice, which is why she reaches out and flicks the lock open. She turns around as I enter, and in her haste to walk away from me, she moves a lot faster than before, no hobbling at all. She's an old faker, Jase's grandma.

"What do you want?" she growls over her shoulder.

"I've just come from the police station," I say. "Jase has been arrested for his father's death. Because the jury found him guilty. You know that, right? You were there at the inquest. You must have heard everything. Including the part where they found fibers of his dad's clothes in the wheelbarrow that was used to take his body to the lake."

She lowers herself into an armchair with the help of her cane.

"My grandmother hired a solicitor for Jase," I continue. "The police just advised me that Jase should tell them everything that happened the night his father died. No one believed the story he told at the inquest, that he and you went to bed and didn't see anything out of the ordinary."

Her mouth tightens up like a drawstring purse.

"But I just don't believe Jase had anything to do with his dad's death." I shove my hands into my pockets, fiddling with their contents. "Mainly because he wouldn't have tried to cover it up if he had. Jase isn't talking because he's protecting someone. That seems really obvious to me."

I have to admire her self-control; she still doesn't say a word.

"I wondered whether it was his mother," I say, and watch a small smile creep over her lips. "But then I realized it couldn't be her. She loves Jase. There's no way she'd stand by and see him arrested for something she did. She's at the police station right now. Waiting to see him. Unlike you."

I stare at her as hard as I can. "There's only one other person who could have killed Mr. Barnes who Jase would protect. One other person who couldn't move the body on their own and could pressure Jase to help them. You."

Even now that I'm directly accusing her, she stays resolutely silent. Jase's grandmother really is as tough as old boots.

"The marks on Mr. Barnes's face, and his legs." I point to her cane. "That's what caused them, isn't it? You hit him and he fell down and cracked his head."

"How could I have done that?" she snaps, her eyes glittering in triumph. "My back's locked up. I can't even bend over to tie my own shoelaces! How could I have swiped Kevin on the legs? And even if I did, he'd just have got up and belted me. Maybe it was Jase! Did you think of that, Miss Clever Clogs? Maybe my grandson took my cane and hit his own father!"

She's right. No way could she have hit stocky Kevin Barnes hard enough to be sure that he would fall and knock himself out, rather than getting up again full of rage. It would have been much too risky. I turn my head away, frustration surging within me. I was so sure I was right. There was no one else Jase could have been protecting.

And then my gaze falls on the rickety wooden staircase in the center of the cottage, and I have a blinding flash of inspiration.

"You did it when he was coming downstairs," I say. "You stood in the hallway after he'd gone up to bed, and called him to come down. And when he did, you whacked him on the legs with your cane, and knocked him head over heels. He tried to fend you off, but you kept on hitting him. It was late and he'd had a lot to drink. He wouldn't have been able to keep his balance. What did you do, hit him till he fell downstairs and broke his neck?"

She stares at me with such malevolence that I'm very glad she's not fifty years younger. I think if she were, I'd be fighting for my life right now.

"You've got more than one cane, I imagine," I say. "Jase fed the one you used through the wood chipper, didn't he? Because it had his father's blood on it."

"You Wakefields," she says bitterly. "Kings and queens of the castle, coming in here and turning everyone else's lives upside down. You think you know it all, don't you? Well, you don't!"

"I'm right, though, aren't I?" I challenge her.

"All right," she hisses. "I did it! I knocked my own son downstairs. And when Jase came home, I got him to carry Kevin outside and make it look like an accident." She snorts. "He made a right mess of *that*, didn't he? Make you happy, does it, Little Miss Nosy, now you've worked it all out? Kevin was a nasty, nasty drunk, and he was getting worse. He'd say

213

all kinds of things when he was on the whisky, talk about things better left dead and buried. And he wouldn't listen to me when I told him to keep his mouth shut." Her hands, on the top of her cane, clench tight as claws. "It was all very well for *him*, but this is the only home I've got. He wasn't going to bring me down with him and get us kicked out of here. No one's going to put me in an old people's home. I came here as a young bride and I'll leave here in a coffin."

I furrow my brow, desperately trying to work out the deeper meaning of this confession. It's like she's talking in code, and it's the most important thing in the world for me to be able to crack it.

"My grandmother," I say slowly. "She's the only person who could make you leave."

"Pulling all the strings," she says sourly. "Snapping her fingers and making everyone dance to her tune."

Just what she'd like to do, I realize. She'd love to have the power my grandmother has, and she's eaten up with jealousy because she doesn't.

"But why would she kick you out of here, after all these years?" I ask, baffled. "I don't understand."

"I'm not saying another word," she says defiantly. "Not another word."

"But you have to!" I stride across the room and bend over her, close enough to be aware of her old-lady smell: mothballs and lavender-scented talcum powder. "You have to tell the police that it was you! That Jase is covering up for you!"

She shrugs defiantly. And the eyes that gleam up at me through her wire-rimmed glasses are triumphant.

"I don't have to tell those coppers anything," she says,

almost conversationally. "Jason will just have to take care of himself."

She thinks she's won. She thinks she's got away with murder, and let her own grandson take the blame for it.

"No good comes of mixing the races," she mutters. "He looks more like that mother of his than any child of mine."

She's a horrible, awful old woman. I don't want to be cooped up in here with her for another second. I don't know how Jase has borne it all these years.

"And besides, this is all your fault, Scarlett Wakefield," she adds nastily. "It was when Jason started running after you that he and his dad really started going at each other hammer and tongs. Kevin was jealous because his son was getting what he couldn't."

"What on earth are you talking about?" I'm even more baffled.

"He saw you and Jason and he couldn't bear it. All those years, thinking about what might have happened if things had gone the way he wanted. And then his son mooning after the heir to Wakefield, the two of you all hearts and flowers. Made him sick to his stomach."

"You mean my mother?" I say, my hand rising to touch the necklace that was once hers. "Did he give this to my mother—this necklace?"

Jase's grandmother doesn't answer me. She just smiles evilly, looking at the necklace, clearly recognizing it but refusing to comment. It's all too obvious that she's deliberately made those references to my mother and Jase's father, thrown the cat among the pigeons to upset me as much as she can.

Focus on what's most important right now, I tell myself firmly. *Saving Jase from the police. She's trying to distract you from what you came here to do. Don't let her get away with it.*

I take a deep breath.

"You're going to ring the police right now and confess," I tell her. "And I'm going to watch you do it."

She laughs in my face.

"Oh, I am, am I?" she says sarcastically. "And who's going to make me? You and whose army?"

I still can't believe she's going to let Jase go to prison for something she did. As I stare at her incredulously, she adds:

"What if I made you promise you'd never see him again? Would you agree to that, Miss Scarlett Wakefield?" Her eyes narrow at me. "Would you give him up if I told you it was the only way to get me to confess?"

I shake my head. "No, I wouldn't."

"Well, then you don't really love him, do you! Banging on to me about that silly mare Dawn and how much she loves him and all the rest of it!" She's enjoying this so much she thumps her cane on the floor in emphatic amusement. "If you *loved* him, you'd jump at the chance to clear his name, wouldn't you? Whatever you had to do!"

"But I don't have to," I say. "I've got your confession already."

And out of my jacket pocket I pull the mobile phone that I retrieved from my locker. When I was fiddling in my pockets, I was turning the video mode on. It's been recording ever since.

Jase's grandmother stares at it blankly, and I realize that she knows practically nothing about modern technology. So I stop the recording, save it, and click the Play button. There's no video on the screen, of course, it's just black: nothing to see inside my jacket pocket. But the sound quality is really good. We listen to the conversation, hypnotized by the sound of our own voices, the gravity of what we're saying. We both hear her admit:

"All right. I did it! I knocked my own son downstairs. And when Jase came home, I got him to carry Kevin outside and make it look like an accident!"

"It would look a lot better if you ring the police and tell them yourself," I say quietly, clicking the Stop button.

"You'll regret this if you make me do it," she says ominously. "I'm warning you, Miss Scarlett Wakefield. You'll regret it. You think you're doing your boyfriend a favor, don't you? Believe me, you're not. You're causing him more trouble than you can even imagine."

I know I should ignore her. I know I should. But I can't.

"What do you mean?" I say, hating myself for asking the question.

Her laugh is the closest thing to a cackle that I've ever heard.

"You'll find out. And you won't like it, believe me. If you make me tell the coppers what I did, it'll all come down on your own head in the end. You'll regret ever starting this with me. Oh yes, you will!"

She raises a hand and points at me malevolently.

"You just leave well alone. Jase won't be in that much

217

trouble, not when I tell the court how his dad used to go after him with a belt. Everyone in Wakefield knows what Kevin was like. He'll just get a slap on the wrist, that's all."

"No!" I say furiously. I have to think about Jase rather than myself. I have to pretend her threats are meaningless to me. "He'll be *convicted*. He'll go to prison. He'll have a record for the rest of his life. I don't care what you say, I won't let that happen to him! You ring the police right now and tell them what really happened, or I'll go to the station and play them this."

I brandish the phone at her furiously. She meets my eyes, and I can see she knows I won't be swayed by anything she might say. With a long sigh, she heaves herself to her feet and hobbles theatrically across the room to the phone. I watch her as she picks up the handset, dials 999, and asks for the police when the operator responds.

"Put me through to the Wakefield police station," she says heavily. "I've got something I need to get off my chest."

I haven't even heard a car pull up outside; I've been so absorbed with the tension of this conversation with Jase's grandmother. It's a complete shock when the door swings open and I see Jase walk in, his solicitor just behind him.

He looks from me to his grandmother, his jaw dropping. I hold up a hand to tell him to keep quiet as his grandmother says:

"It's Dorothy Barnes here. Kevin Barnes's mum. I want to confess to killing my son, though I was just protecting myself. He came for me that night and I hit him off to keep him away from me, and he fell downstairs and broke his sorry drunken neck. I got Jase to put him outside, but that's all he did, and that's the truth."

Jase's eyes are wide as saucers.

"Yes, I'm at home," she says. "Yes, I'll be here. Where do you think I'm going at my age? On the run?" She snorts and hangs up the phone.

"It was self-defense," she says firmly, plopping herself back into her chair once more. "An old woman like me, with my drunken son on the rampage. I had to protect myself, didn't I? It wasn't like my grandson was here to look after me and make his dad keep his hands to himself!"

· *She'll get away with it,* I think. *She'll stick to that story and she'll get away with it. There's no way they'll put an old lady on trial and try to send her to prison.*

Jas Ramu is staring at Jase's grandmother in amazement. She starts to say something, but Mrs. Barnes hasn't finished.

"And now, I've got something to tell you, before they come to take me away," she says, staring at Jase. "You probably don't want your girlfriend hearing this, I'm warning you. It's about your dad, and it's as bad as it can be. Now that he's gone, it's time for you to hear it all."

I look frantically at Jase.

"Go, Scarlett," he says between gritted teeth.

"But, Jase—"

"Please," he says desperately, "*go!*"

His grandmother cackles again.

"That's right. You get out while you can, Scarlett Wakefield. You know, it's actually a relief to be telling the truth, after all these years?" she adds. "Ooh, I've got a *lot* to get off my chest!"

The next thing I know, Jase has grabbed me. He's almost frog-marching me across the room, pushing me out the door, his jaw set.

"*Jase!*" I exclaim, completely shocked at being man-handled.

"I'll ring you," he says quickly, "really soon. Don't fight me on this, Scarlett. Please just *go!*"

As the door shuts behind me, I stand on the steps to the cottage and listen to his grandmother laugh and laugh, like she's just heard the best joke in the world. Then I realize something.

I'm actually grateful that Jase just bundled me out of the door in such a hurry. Because, seasoned detective though I am by now, there's no way that I want to hear precisely what his grandmother's about to reveal to him so gloatingly.

Twenty-Two

"PILLOWCASE OR SCISSORS?"

I have to walk. Somewhere, anywhere. My legs are moving on their own, taking me off, away from the cottage and what's unfolding inside. It's a survival mechanism, my body taking care of my mind, making sure it doesn't overload completely. I'm in a glass bubble, closed off from the world, unable to process one more item of information.

Cold air on my face. Hard concrete under my feet. My heart, pumping loudly in my chest. The distant cries of younger girls playing on the stone terraces behind the main school building.

Wow. If girls are throwing balls and jumping rope on the terraces, school must be finished for the day. I glance at my watch: yup, four-thirty. I don't know where the time has gone. It's like my life is jumping in huge leaps from one shocking revelation to another, rather than the normal slow, boring routine of my daily existence at Wakefield Hall—lessons, studying, working out, punctuated with spikes of excitement (Jase) or confrontation (Plum).

I look back to the time when all Jase and I had to worry

about was his father yelling and chasing us. In retrospect, it seems like a golden age of ease and relaxation.

My feet have carried me through the parking lot, around the new wing and to the entrance to Pankhurst dormitory. I realize that they're taking me to Taylor's room. Well, my feet know what I need better than my brain does. Even if Taylor isn't there, which I hope she is, I can curl up on her bed, text her to come and find me, put on some music, make myself a hot chocolate from her stash, and take refuge from the rest of the world without having to go back to Aunt Gwen's.

There's no one on the back stairs of the dormitory, which is a huge relief. I make it up the three flights to the Sixth Form floor and down the corridor. Some of the doors are ajar, music or computer noise streaming out. In the common room a group of girls are watching *Music and Lyrics* for the umpteenth time, a romantic comedy with Drew Barrymore and Hugh Grant that has become the comfort food of the autumn term. Lizzie, who has predictably gone more mad for it than anyone else, has been singing the songs from it for weeks now. I assume she's in there, driving everyone else crazy, piping away in her high-pitched soprano.

But I'm very wrong there. Because as I approach Taylor's room, the door closed as always (Taylor is never going to win a Miss Congeniality contest), I hear Lizzie's trademark nervous, squeaky giggle from behind it.

Lizzie in Taylor's room? That's strange. I instantly picture Lizzie giving Taylor tips on manicures and leg waxing techniques, or Taylor making Lizzie watch American football online while she explains to her interminably why they keep stopping and starting all the time. (Even I refuse to do that with her, despite the fact that I quite like the guys' shiny Lycra leggings.)

I push the door open, suddenly very curious as to what exactly might be going on inside Taylor's private sanctum.

Nothing, literally nothing, could have prepared me for what I see inside.

It must be a practical joke. A really twisted, weird practical joke played by someone with a very underdeveloped sense of humor.

Crowded round Taylor's computer are Lizzie, Susan, and Plum. Given how much Taylor does not like company, I'm absolutely stunned to see them here. In fact, it's kind of like walking in on my grandmother and Mr. Barnes smoking cigars and doing tequila shots.

"What did I tell you, ladies?" Plum's trilling as she clicks on the screen. "Aren't these photos to *die* for? Oh my God. Look at *this* one. It looks like a bunch of lesbos in an Ugliest Butch contest!"

I sneak a look over her arm. The image is of Taylor and a cluster of girls wearing bright yellow and green tops, jumping up to a hoop at a basketball game. Honestly, I'm beginning to think that this harping on about lesbians has more to do with Plum than with Taylor. All I see in that photo is a bunch of sporty, sweaty girls with big legs and bigger grimaces. I mean, they're not grabbing each other's boobs instead of the ball, are they?

But where's Taylor? My God, if they've sneaked into her room to spy on her behind her back, she's going to go nuclear on them when she returns. Their lives will literally not be worth living.

And then, half hidden behind them, I see a fourth figure, sitting on the bed. It's unmistakeably Taylor. I recognize the wide shoulders and the white T-shirt immediately.

I don't identify her by her face. I can't. Because pulled down over it, covering even her neck, is one of her own pillowcases.

A red mist floods my eyes. It doesn't blind me completely, though, because how else could I storm across the room, shove Susan aside, grab hold of the pillowcase, and drag it off Taylor's head? How else could I see that, unbelievably, the pillowcase isn't tied or taped or fastened in any way, meaning that there's no reason Taylor couldn't just yank it off herself? How else could I reach to the shelf behind her, snatch a pair of scissors out of the Cornell mug in which Taylor keeps all her pens and markers, and, holding the pillowcase in one hand and the scissors in the other, turn to confront Plum, Susan, and Lizzie, with an expression that must be so menacing that Lizzie actually falls back, whimpering in fear?

"What is going on here?" I demand furiously.

"Scarlett! Such a flair for the dramatic!" Plum says quickly, recovering from the initial shock I'm sure I saw in her eyes. "I thought you had more than enough of that going on in your own life right now."

"Who put this over Taylor's head?" I'm so angry I think I can taste blood.

"We shouldn't have," Susan wails. "I knew we shouldn't have, but—"

"Was it you?" I point at her. Her blue eyes widen and I see her swallowing, too paralyzed by fear to speak.

"Why don't you ask Taylor?" Plum cuts in, smiling now with anticipation. "That should clear things up for you."

I look over at Taylor. She's pushing her tangled hair off her face; it must have been hot under the pillowcase. Her mouth is set in a hard straight line, her brows drawn together. She looks angry enough to punch someone in the face.

I don't understand why she's still just sitting there. Why she isn't jumping to her feet, picking Plum, Susan, and Lizzie up one by one and throwing them out the door.

And even less do I understand when she mumbles to me, "I put it on, Scarlett."

"What?"

"I put the pillowcase on myself."

"I suggested she might want to," Plum adds, leaning back in Taylor's desk chair and crossing her legs at the ankles. "So she didn't get in the way while we were looking at her photographs."

This is insane. I take a deep breath, restoring some degree of self-control. *Come on, it's obvious what's happening. Plum has much more of a hold over Taylor than you realized.* And Plum is enjoying herself immensely flaunting it.

This can't go on. I won't let it.

I advance on Plum, who still has a taunting smile on her lips. She seems absolutely sure that she's invulnerable. That there's nothing I can do to touch her, because she's made it clear that she controls Taylor, and if I hurt her, Taylor will suffer for it.

She's gone too far now. This is war.

I reach out and grab hold of Plum's hair, twisting her

ponytail around my left hand, pulling her up till her back's straight.

"I'm going to give you a choice," I say icily as she shrieks in protest. "Either you put that pillowcase on your head, right now, just like Taylor did, or I'm cutting your hair off."

I brandish the scissors.

"You know I'll do it. Look in my eyes. Put that pillowcase on right now, or I'll start cutting."

"Scarlett," Lizzie moans in protest. "You can't! Not her hair!"

Still holding Plum's ponytail in an iron grip, I glance over at Lizzie and Susan, who are huddling together against the far wall, their faces as frightened as if they were watching someone being disemboweled in a 3-D horror film.

"You know Jase Barnes is my boyfriend, right?" I say to them. "You know his dad died the other day and there were police around?"

They nod in unison, their eyes so big I can see the whites all round their irises.

"Plum told the police that Jase and I were together," I inform them. "Jase got in huge trouble because of what she said."

It's the cardinal sin, the worst thing one girl can do to another. Cutting off Plum's hair would be infinitely less culpable in our moral lexicon than tattling on her to someone in authority—a teacher, a parent, let alone a police officer. Susan's beautiful face and Lizzie's overly made-up one are identical masks of incredulity as they turn to stare at Plum, who is squirming and huffing but not uttering a word.

"You can't trust her," I say with infinite satisfaction, knowing that I've landed a killer blow. "You think if you stick with her you'll be safe, don't you? You think it's better to be on her side, even if that means doing something as shitty and mean as bullying someone and laughing at her photos. But it isn't. Plum will turn on you any time she wants to. If she can sneak on someone to the police, she's capable of anything."

I can't see Plum's face. But the way Susan and Lizzie are staring at her with repulsion must mean my words are having their effect. I'm sure my own expression is vindictive beyond belief. I feel like I'm snarling down at her.

"Get out," I say, nodding brusquely toward the door. "No, wait. Apologize to Taylor, and then get out."

They tumble over each other to stutter their "sorry's" at Taylor and scramble out the door.

"Pillowcase or scissors?" I ask Plum.

"Piss off," she hisses at me, trying to twist away and yelping in pain as I pull back on her ponytail.

"Right, then," I say. "Scissors it is."

"No!" Plum screams.

"Don't do it, Scarlett," Taylor says grimly.

"She can't get away with this." I know that if Plum isn't stopped now, things will escalate to a degree that I can't possibly fathom.

"Please!" Plum begs. "Not my hair!"

It's awful how much I enjoy hearing her grovel. Power really does corrupt. I let her ponytail go, step back, and hold out the pillowcase to her. Silently, her eyes narrowed slits of rage, she takes it and pulls it down over her head. I take the bottom corners and knot them tightly enough so she won't get it off in a hurry. Then I grab her shoulders and frog-march her out of the room.

227

After which I yell, "Hey, everyone! Plum's trying out a new Halloween costume!" loudly enough so that throngs of girls come out of their rooms all down the corridor, and out of the common room. They stare in amazement at Plum tottering as she tries desperately to wrest the pillowcase up and over her head.

Once one girl starts to giggle, it starts a chain reaction, and soon everyone is laughing at Plum. I don't feel a shred of sympathy whatsoever.

"Somebody help me!" she screams, tugging so hard on the pillowcase that she pulls on her chin, overbalances, trips, and slams into the wall.

Lizzie and Susan are in the crowd, looking at each other. Some silent communication takes place between them. I notice that neither of them steps forward to help Plum. It's Sharon Persaud who finally steadies Plum's shoulders and starts helping her off with the pillowcase while everyone else keeps laughing hysterically.

I shut the door and turn to confront Taylor. I place my hands on my hips and stare at her sternly.

"Will you *please* tell me what the hell is going on between you and Plum?"

. . .

Taylor is slumped on the bed, looking drained. Her hair is sweaty from being pasted down. Without a word, she stands up and walks over to the computer, scrolling through the photos.

I remember Plum's comments about Taylor and the basketball girls. I brace myself for what Taylor might be about to show me. My guess is some picture of her kissing a girl.

Suddenly, with a flash of insight into my own motives, I think: *So what? So what if she's kissing a girl?* And then I realize why I may have been so confused about the entire idea.

It's not because I'm freaking out that Taylor might be gay. It's because I hate the idea that Plum might know more about my best friend than I do.

This revelation is such a big relief that my limbs go all loose and floppy. I even hear myself giggle a little, a silly titter of release.

"What's so funny?" Taylor asks incredulously over her shoulder.

"Nothing," I say quickly. "I'm just so wound up with everything that's been going on. It was just a nervous thing."

And then I see what she's been searching for on the screen, and my eyes widen. This is not at all what I was expecting.

"Okay," I say slowly.

It's an older, male version of Taylor. Dark shaggy hair, pale skin, green-gray eyes under dark brows. Taylor's high cheekbones are unmistakable, but the square jaw, the dark stubble, are unequivocally manly. He's frowning, just like Taylor. And he's a few years older, closer to a man than a boy.

"Let me guess," I say. "A distant relative?"

"Funny," Taylor says with a faint trace of a smile.

No question that this is Taylor's brother, Seth. The one who goes to Cornell University in America. I had no idea they were that alike.

"What does this have to do with Plum?" I ask, totally bewildered.

Taylor heaves a long sigh, and swivels her chair round to face me.

"You know this winter Plum went to Venice?"

"Of course I know she went to Venice," I say, rolling my eyes. "She's been banging on about it ever since. Those bloody glass bracelets that she never stops playing with. 'Murano glass, of course, hand-blown!'" I mimic Plum viciously.

"That was all about sending me a message," Taylor says, lowering her voice. "Keeping me in line so I didn't talk back when she was picking a fight with you."

I stare at her blankly, not understanding.

"Tonight wasn't the first time Plum was looking at photos on my computer. I don't know how she did it, but she snuck into my room when I wasn't here and rifled through my digital photo albums," Taylor says.

"Why am I not surprised?" I comment dryly.

"Anyway, Plum saw pictures of me and Seth from a couple years ago. So when she saw him in Venice at a high-society party, she asked the hostess if she could be introduced to Seth. But when the hostess brought Plum over to Seth, she said his name was Will Michaels, heir to some fortune."

I furrow my brow, still completely in the dark. Why would Seth need to hide his true identity?

"So of course," Taylor continues, "that totally set Plum off. She called him on his BS and she said, in front of everyone, that he was my brother and he was lying about who he was. But he kept on denying it."

"Is he in some kind of trouble?"

"You could say that," Taylor says in the voice you use when you're making a gigantic understatement. "After Plum blew his cover, he had to get out of Venice and abort the entire, um, mission."

"*Cover? Mission?*" I honestly can't believe what I'm hearing.

Taylor takes a deep breath.

"Scarlett, you know how I told you that my folks are archaeologists?"

I nod. "They're on a dig in Turkey."

"Well, that's a cover story too. They work for a government agency. And so does my brother. It's like a family thing."

"You mean they're *spies*?" I gasp.

Taylor winces.

"We never use that word," she said hastily. "My parents hate it. But, um, pretty much, yeah, it's sort of in that general vicinity."

I stare at her, mesmerized. This is probably why Taylor has been training so hard—not to be a PI, but to work undercover for the government someday.

This is the definition of surreal.

"Plum knows something big was up in Venice," Taylor continues. "The first chance she got, she started dogging me about it."

"You should have told me before," I say reproachfully. "I can totally keep a secret. And I could have helped you come up with a plan to fend her off."

Taylor sighs, long and hard. "She threatened to sic one of her *Tatler* reporter friends on the story of Will Michaels, mysteriously vanishing millionaire. If the *Tatler* printed something like that, it could so easily lead back to my mom and dad. And that wouldn't just be the end of their careers. It could actually put them in danger."

My heart lodges in my throat. I know what it's like to be hounded by journalists. I had that experience after Dan's death. I wouldn't wish it on anyone, except for my worse enemy.

Now Taylor is choking back tears. "I could see the way you looked at me when Plum would say things and I wouldn't react. It drove me nuts. I so wanted to tell you, Scarlett. But you know, this is a huge secret, and it's not just mine. When I talked to Seth about it, he was totally, totally against me saying a word to you. He doesn't trust anyone outside the family, and he's my big brother. I couldn't go against him."

Seth sounds like a bossy twat, I think. But then again, he's only trying to protect his family. I suppose I get that.

"Well, it's obvious what we need to do now, isn't it?" I say firmly.

Taylor stares at me.

"*Is* it?" she asks.

"Oh yeah," I say. "We need to get some deep, dark dirt on Plum. Whatever her worst secret is, we need to find it. Then we'll have some serious leverage."

I give Taylor a long, wondering look as she sits there, contemplating my suggestion.

"I still can't quite get my head round all of this about your family," I admit. "I mean, I wouldn't believe a word of it if it wasn't you telling me."

"Scarlett? Are you still there? Scarlett?"

It's Lizzie's high, fluting voice, sounding more nervous than ever. She's tapping on the door convulsively with her knuckles, like a woodpecker with OCD.

"Scarlett!" Her voice rises even higher. "Scarlett!"

232

"Oh, just let her in and we'll get it over with," Taylor says with resignation.

I go to the door and ease it open a crack.

"What is it?" I say angrily. "Don't you think you've bothered Taylor enough for one day?"

Lizzie's face crumples.

"I'm so sorry," she moans. "I knew it was wrong. But Plum just makes you do things. . . ."

"Forget it," Taylor says. "Seriously."

I start to close the door.

"Wait!" Lizzie says urgently. "I just want to tell you something. It's important."

"Okay, but make it quick," I say.

She points at my collarbones. I look down, and realize that she's gesturing at my pendant, which is still hanging outside the neckline of my sweater.

"It's about your necklace. That's *not* an aquamarine, believe me. I've seen all my mum's stuff that my dad's keeping for me, and I've got some good pieces of my own. I know precious stones." Her words are tumbling over each other, she's talking so quickly. "Scarlett, that's a round-cut blue diamond. It's really, really rare."

I gape at her.

"And obviously, that means it's incredibly valuable," Lizzie emphasizes, in the tone of a self-made billionaire's daughter who takes jewelry very seriously indeed. "How could you not know you had a *round-cut, brilliant blue diamond* round your neck?"

Twenty-three

WAKEFIELD BLUE

"So both of you want to see Lady Wakefield?" Penny asks, looking from me to Taylor.

"Um, I'm not sure," I mutter.

Clearly, decision-making is pretty much beyond my range of available skills at the moment. The apocalyptically huge events of today have burnt out that part of my brain. I still haven't got anywhere near to processing Taylor's family secret. I mean, you know there are spies, obviously. Not just in films, but in real life, too. But you never think you're going to meet someone who's related to several. Though, thinking about it, anyone more likely than Taylor to be a spy-in-training, with her investigative skills, toughness, and loner personality, would be hard to find.

"Maybe talking to your grandmother isn't the best idea in the world," Taylor suggests. "No offense, Scarlett, but you need to be totally on the ball when you meet with her, and you're kind of coming across like a boiled vegetable right now."

Penny raises a hand to cover her smile. She's very well mannered.

"I must say, Miss McGovern does have a point," she says, positioning her pince-nez more firmly on her nose. "Would you like to make an appointment for tomorrow, perhaps? Is this about young Jason Barnes?"

I shake my head.

"It's not really about Jase."

My grandmother will hear all about the Barnes family drama soon enough from Jase's solicitor, Jas Ramu. I just don't feel up to giving Penny a sketch of the latest developments, and having to deal with all her consequent shock, disbelief, and sympathy.

I glance down at Penny, who's seated behind her desk, which is a delicate, late-eighteenth-century, with elegantly slim, curved legs and an elaborately inlaid top. It would make anyone larger than a waif look hulking by comparison, but Penny has the bones of a bird. She can wear old-fashioned tweed suits with twinsets underneath and still look tiny. She's been working for my grandmother ever since Lady Wakefield turned the Hall into a girls' school, and, in true aristocratic style, she's probably wearing the same tweed suits now as she did over forty years ago, when the school was founded.

A thoughtful light is shining in Penny's eyes, behind the lenses of her gold-framed pince-nez.

"I don't suppose it's anything I could help with?" she asks.

It can't hurt, I think.

"It's about this," I say, leaning forward a little to show Penny the pendant.

235

"My goodness!" she exclaims, one hand fluttering up to touch it for a second. "Your mother's necklace! Oh, I remember that so well." She sighs. "Oh dear, that does bring back memories. So sad."

"When did she get it?"

Penny looks amazed.

"You don't know, Scarlett? It was given to her by your father on your fourth birthday. To match the color of your eyes. People said they would fade—sometimes that bright blue doesn't last beyond a couple of years with babies, you know. But your mother always said your eyes would stay that color. She called it Wakefield blue. It was a joke between them. And on your fourth birthday, he gave her that necklace as a present. A Wakefield blue diamond."

There's a lump in my throat as big as a tennis ball. I can't speak.

"Should you be wearing that out, though?" Penny asks, her brow creasing into hundreds of tiny little horizontal lines. "It's terribly valuable. Why isn't it in the jewelry safe?"

"It was lost," Taylor says, since I still can't say a word. "Scarlett found it."

"Really?" Penny's brow creases still further. "I really do feel it ought to be kept in the safe, Scarlett."

"Not just yet." I wrap my hand around the pendant as if Penny is going to try to wrench it off my neck.

"You poor girl," Penny says softly. "Well, come and find me if you ever change your mind."

Penny is a fervent protector of everything Wakefield, so meticulous and proper that my grandmother has absolutely no hesitation giving her a writing desk for daily use that's probably worth a small fortune too. I know it goes against every instinct she has to let me leave her office with a Wakefield diamond hanging around my neck, rather than safely locked away, and I'm more grateful to her than I can say for not pressing the point.

"So your dad gave it to your mom on your fourth birthday," Taylor says as we walk down the corridor. "Which is . . . ?"

"April tenth," I say automatically.

"Right. And she had it that summer, at the village fete, because you saw it in the newspaper photo. So sometime between the fete and her dying, Mr. Barnes got hold of it and gave it to his wife." She shakes her head. "That just makes no sense at all."

"Could my mother have given it to Mr. Barnes?" I speculate, though I hate even to say the words.

"Why would she have done that? I mean, given him anything at all, let alone something that pricey?" Taylor asks with her usual common sense.

I clear my throat, which has suddenly become dry and scratchy. "I think they might have been—involved in some way."

I could barely get those words out.

"Your mom and Mr. Barnes?" Taylor looks so astonished I nearly burst out laughing.

"Jase says his dad was really good-looking when he was younger," I say. "And Aunt Gwen and Jase's grandmother hinted about him and her."

Taylor pulls a face.

"Your mom? With the groundskeeper? I don't believe it. Remember that photo of you with your folks at the village

237

fete? They were so happy. They were, like, beaming! No way was anything going on with your mom and the help. I mean, she'd have to be insane to pull anything like that."

It's a huge relief to hear this, even if Taylor is wrong. I stop dead and enfold her in a gigantic hug, and to my great surprise, she actually hugs me back just as hard, which is very unlike her.

"Thanks for this afternoon," she mumbles into my ear. "I couldn't have done it myself. She's been riding me for so long, and it's been getting worse and worse."

"You can't let Plum own you," I say firmly. "We'll sort this out together."

"Together," Taylor says, pulling back a little and bumping fists with me. Then, without meaning to, she does a comical double-take: her eyebrows shoot up and her mouth falls open as she realizes something she'd completely forgotten.

"Ohmigod, Scarlett. I'm so sorry! I didn't even ask you what's happening with Jase!"

I grimace at how crazy this day's turned out to be.

"Let's go back to your room and lock the door, and I'll tell you everything, okay?" I hesitate for a moment, and then, bravely, because Taylor really doesn't do sentimental or slushy, I add:

"I don't know what I'd do without you, Taylor. I really don't. You're the best friend I could possibly have."

"Shut up," Taylor says gruffly. But she hugs me again, a quick rough hug that's more like being squeezed by a bear.

"Same for me, okay?" She lets me go and heads off down the corridor, her shoulders back, her stride more confident than ever.

As if she's determined to show the world that she's not at all the kind of girl who would ever do anything as soppy as hug her best friend in public. Twice.

• • •

Jase doesn't ring me till nearly nine that evening. I've been waiting and waiting for his call, but after last time, I know better than to ring him or, worse, go to see him when he's told me he needs to be by himself. I'm really trying to be mature. I know that talk with his grandmother must have been unbelievably horrendous, judging by the kind of nastiness she was prepared to spew out to me. And seeing her taken away by the police . . . well, if he needs time after that, I completely understand.

Taylor agreed, which was a relief, because all I know about boys you could write on the back of a postage stamp and still have quite a lot of space left over. She said that when Seth goes off on his own, in a sulk or just to have some thinking time, she's learned to leave him alone.

"I just let him, like, go into his cave and get his head together," she explained. "It's like this process he has to go through on his own. But when he comes out of it, he's always really happy to see me, and thankful for the space."

Even with all my good resolutions, though, I don't know how much longer I could have held out without at least texting Jase to ask if he was okay. I almost cry with relief at the sound of his voice, though I do my best not to let that show.

He asks me to come over to the cottage, saying his grandmother isn't there. He sounds exhausted, but I try not to read too much into that. I'm down the drainpipe almost in a flash. It's getting easier and easier the more I do it. If this keeps up, in a couple of weeks, I'll be more used to scaling the pipe to go home in the evening than walking in the front door and going up the stairs.

The door of the cottage is open a crack. I hesitate on the steps for a second or two, unable to believe it's okay for me to go inside. I still half expect Jase's grandmother to come hobbling into the doorway and brandish her cane at me, yelling at me to go away and never come back.

Finally, I push the door farther open, and walk inside a few paces.

Then I freeze. Jase is coming down the stairs, a bulging gym bag slung over his shoulder. It isn't zipped up yet, and a sleeve of his favorite red sweater is trailing out from the opening.

I know exactly what's going on. And it makes me panic.

"No!" I say instantly, in complete and utter denial.

"Scarlett," he begins.

"No! You can't just go!"

Jase drops the gym bag to the floor.

"Let's sit down for a moment, okay?" he says, taking my hands and pulling me toward the sofa.

It's very old and very saggy. We sink into it till our bottoms hit the ancient springs below. Jase and I wriggle to face each other. He's holding my hands tightly, and the warmth of his fingers calms me down a bit, though I'm still glancing over at the gym bag as if it's a bomb about to go off.

"What happened with your grandmother?" I ask nervously, staring into his face, trying to read it for clues. He looks very tired. His usually caramel skin has that ashy tinge it gets when he's working too hard and not getting enough sleep.

"The coppers came and took her off to the police station," he says wearily. "That solicitor woman went with her. She says she doesn't think my gran'll have to do any time. They'll give her probation, because, you know, she's really old and no one thinks she'll re-offend."

"I don't know," I say. "I can see your gran going on a mini–crime spree all over Wakefield, terrorizing everyone with her cane. Can't you?"

I'm desperately trying to cheer us up with a pathetic attempt at humor, and it does actually make him crack a small smile.

"I wouldn't put it past her," he says wryly. Then he sighs. "Still, if she gets probation, it means that she'll be coming back here to live." He nods around him, indicating the cottage. "It's her home, you know? But I can't stay with her."

I hadn't thought about this at all.

"No, you can't," I admit reluctantly. "But there's bound to be somewhere else on the estate you can live. My grandmother said lots of nice things about you to me when you were arrested. I'm sure she'll be happy to help. Then you can do what you planned—live and work here while you go to college."

Jase starts at the local college in Havisham next autumn. He wants to be a landscape gardener, and the careers officer at his school advised him to get an estate management and gardening degree first. He's really excited about it.

"I don't know, Scarlett." He looks away from me. "I don't

think I can stay at Wakefield. Not after everything that's gone on here."

"But, Jase—"

"Look, the last thing I want is to tell you this, okay?" he blurts out, his voice cracking with strain. "It's horrible. I still can't believe it. But my gran told me . . . she told me that my—my dad . . ." He stammers. "Scarlett, look, I can't think of a good way to say this, right? I'm so sorry. So sorry. But she told me that my dad killed your mum and dad."

Thank God I suspected this already, I think, with some small clear part of my mind. I think of all the evidence I found that pointed to Jase's dad's involvement in their deaths—the news articles that Taylor and I found, the chipping paint on Dawn's van, my mom's pendant. If I hadn't put these pieces together over the past few weeks, if I didn't have more than an idea of the truth already, I honestly think I would faint dead away, or go completely stark staring mad.

Then again, the night is still young.

I look down at our hands, which are still joined.

"She didn't say it was an accident?" I ask in a tiny voice.

Jase shakes his head.

"I'm so sorry," he says again, his lower lip trembling. "She said that was why he didn't want me seeing you."

Finally, he registers the way I'm reacting to this disastrous news.

"You don't sound that surprised," he says, very taken aback. "I thought this would be the worst shock in the world."

"I had some idea already," I admit. "My parents were hit by a white van, for instance, and that old one your mum drives? It's blue, but you can see where it's all bashed up that there was white paint underneath."

Jase closes his eyes.

"And the way your dad was toward me," I continue. "There had to be some deeper reason for that. It never made sense that he was so angry that you and I were boyfriend and girlfriend."

"No, it never did." Jase squeezes my hands. "It never did."

I start crying, very slowly at first. Then Jase's eyes snap open.

"Why would he do something like that?" he asks hopelessly. "And why would he stay on here at Wakefield Hall afterward? My gran said that's what drove him to drink, but for all these years, I've been told it was my mum who did that."

I sniff, and pull my hands away to wipe my face.

"Scarlett, I'm so sorry my family has hurt yours so badly," he says. "I don't know if anything I can do will ever make it up to you."

He hugs me clumsily, our bodies squashing together in the dip of the saggy sofa.

"Which is why I can't stay here," he says, kissing my forehead. "Now that I know it's true." He shivers. "To be honest, I didn't even know whether to believe my gran or not. She's such a miserable old bag. You wouldn't believe the stuff she's thrown at me over the years."

Oh yes, I would, I think, remembering all the racist things she's said to me.

He takes a deep breath.

"I've been trying to make sense of everything myself," he says. "I think Mum insisted on taking the van when she left as insurance, in a way. Maybe she did know what my dad had done. She'd never have had the nerve to stand up to him and tell him directly. Taking the van'd have been a sort of round-the-house way of saying it, making sure he wouldn't come after her."

I nod slowly, thinking of scared, frail Dawn. Jase's theory makes complete sense.

"And your grandmother knew too," I say.

"Clearly." He smiles—a smile without any humor whatsoever. "She's a real charmer, my gran, isn't she? Didn't mind what her son had done, or not enough to do a sodding thing about it. It was only when you and I started seeing each other, and my dad went into meltdown, that she lifted a finger. And that was just to save herself."

He looks seriously at me.

"She knocked him down the stairs to keep the house, you know," he tells me. "It was all about her. She thought if Dad kept going as he was—getting more and more drunk and out of control—your grandma would tell him he had to leave the Hall, and that she'd make my gran go too."

"My grandmother would never kick an old lady out of her home," I say with absolute conviction.

"What can I say?" Jase shrugs. "I don't think she would either. But you know the thing about my gran? When you're as nasty and evil as she is, you judge everyone against yourself. My gran thinks everyone's like her, and that means she always expects the worst."

I nod, recognizing that he's right.

"I went to see Lady Wakefield this evening," Jase says, which makes me pull back and look at him in great surprise.

244

"It's okay, don't worry. I had to thank her for getting me a solicitor. She was really nice. She wouldn't hear of me paying her back for any of it, and said she didn't blame me for anything. And that there'd be a job for me here as long as I wanted it. You were right there. She'd let me stay on if I wanted." He hesitates for a moment. "She doesn't know why my gran did it. No one does but you and me. And the solicitor, but she can't tell because it's confidential with her client. Everyone just thinks my dad raised his hand to my gran, and she was defending herself. And then she panicked and got me to try to cover it up. No one knows about Dad and your parents."

"Good," I say quietly.

Because I'm sure there's more to find out about my parents' death. How did my mother's necklace come into Mr. Barnes's possession? What's behind all the hints from Aunt Gwen and Jase's gran about my mother? Until I solve those mysteries, connect them all together, I'll be positive that I haven't found out the whole truth.

And I don't want the spotlight on me and my parents while Taylor and I are unraveling the clues.

Jase closes his eyes again briefly.

"What's wrong with us, Scarlett? What did we do to deserve this?"

"I don't know," I say sadly. "It's so unfair."

Jase stands up and tears spring to my eyes once more. He walks over to his gym bag, which is lying on the floor.

"I have to take off and get my thoughts straight," he says. "I'm spinning off in circles right now, you know what I mean?"

I do. I know exactly what he means. But holding on to Jase, being close to him, makes me feel like I'm at the center of the circles. Safe. I wish desperately it could be the same for him.

I jump up and run over to him, reaching up to pull his head down and kiss him. But we're both so wound up, so confused, so unhappy, that a proper kiss is completely beyond us.

"Please don't go," I whisper into his ear.

"You know it isn't about you," he says gently as he unwraps his arms from me and drops a light kiss on my lips. "You know I love you."

Tears blur my eyes and slide down my cheeks.

"I love you too."

But though we've said we love each other for the first time, what ought to be the most wonderful moment in our lives actually sounds much more like goodbye.

"I'll talk to you soon," Jase says, picking up his bag and heading for the door.

I nod silently. I sense that if I plead any more, it will only make things worse.

Jacket zipped up, gloves on, gym bag stowed under the seat of the bike, Jase kisses me once again. My face is wet, and he wipes the tears away with his glove.

"I don't know what to say, Scarlett," he admits hopelessly. "It's tearing me up to leave you like this."

"Just promise me you'll come back," I sob, running my fingers through his hair.

"I promise," he says.

And then I have to stand there, watching him put on his helmet, straddle the bike, and start it up. He turns around for one last look at me and to wave goodbye. I wave back and all of a sudden the bike jumps forward and speeds off—around the building, down the back road, dissolving, fading smaller and smaller till at last I can't see the red rear light gleaming in the dark or hear the roar of the bike's engine.

Jase has gone.

I could break into a thousand pieces right now.

My hand rises to the pendant round my neck. The diamond my mother called Wakefield blue. My fingers close around it, and I know what I need to do now.

I need to find out everything about why Jase's father killed my parents.

I'll help Taylor get the dirt on Plum—the dirt Taylor needs to keep her secret safe. And in return, Taylor will help me find out the truth about what happened at Wakefield Hall all those years ago.

And maybe, just maybe, the truth will set Jase and me free.